Hannah Pritchard
Pirate of the Revolution

Bonnie Pryor

Enslow Publishers, Inc.
40 Industrial Road
Box 398
Berkeley Heights, NJ 07922
USA

http://www.enslow.com

*To my grandson, Tyler. He shares his imagined worlds
and sometimes lets me be the pirate.*

Library of Congress Cataloging-in-Publication Data:

Pryor, Bonnie.
    Hannah Pritchard : pirate of the Revolution / Bonnie Pryor.
        p. cm. — (Historical Fiction Adventures (HFA))
    Summary: After her parents and brother are killed by Loyalists, fourteen-year-old
Hannah leaves their farm and eventually, disguised as a boy, joins a pirate ship that preys
on other ships to get supplies for the American Revolution.
    ISBN-13: 978-0-7660-2851-7
    ISBN-10: 0-7660-2851-8
    [1. Pirates—Fiction. 2. United States—History—Revolution, 1775-1783—Fiction.
3. Sex role—Fiction. 4. Sea stories.] I. Title.
PZ7.P94965Han 2007
[Fic]—dc22   2007005302

Printed in the United States of America

10 9 8 7 6 5 4 3 2 1

This is a juvenile fiction book.

Illustration Credits: Original Painting by Corey Wolfe, p. 1; Enslow Publishers, Inc., p. 156; U.S. Department of Defense, p. 158; Reproduced from *Nautical Illustrations*, published by Dover Publications, Inc., pp. 155, 157.

Cover Illustration: Original Painting by Corey Wolfe.

Contents

chapter one

Attack!

The cave was dark. A faint musty odor lingered from generations of small animals that had sheltered there, seeking protection from the fierce winters. Hannah crouched in the farthest corner. So complete was her terror that she scarcely felt the jagged rocks, hard enough to bruise, pressed against her back. Her heart pounded so loudly that she feared it would be heard echoing between the narrow damp stone walls.

Through an opening that was low to the ground and barely large enough to squeeze through, she could see the scuff marks she had made in the dry earth. Her breath caught in her throat in panic. The Iroquois were skilled trackers. They were sure to see the evidence she had left. She forced herself to move, but her foot bumped the half-filled bucket of berries she had brought into the cave with her. The bucket struck the stone wall of the cave with a soft metallic ping. Hannah froze. There was no triumphant yell, no pounding feet to indicate the sound had betrayed her presence. After a minute, she allowed herself to breathe again. Stepping around the bucket, she crouched at the low entrance and peered out. Was she really alone? Or was someone there, just out of sight, waiting for her to show herself?

After a second of hesitation, she pushed herself partially out the entrance. Lying flat, she could reach handfuls of pine needles. Working quickly from her awkward position, she smoothed and patted the dirt and sprinkled the pine needles over the top. Beads of sweat formed on her forehead, although her body was shivering with terror. She hoped she had covered signs of her presence, but the entrance was still exposed. If someone were to bend down and look in, she would be visible. A small bush struggled for life in the rocky soil near the entrance, but it was too well rooted to dislodge.

There wasn't much time left. Hannah could hear the small cracking of branches, the soft thud of footsteps—sounds of men passing through the forest. With a strength fueled by desperation, she managed to break the main stem so that the bush covered the opening. She shrank back against the stone walls of her shelter. Through the leafy cover of the bush, she could see feet, the soft silent moccasins of warriors and the more measured tread of the soldiers' boots. By crouching down, she could see flashes of red and green jackets—British and Tory soldiers. And so many! This wasn't a small raiding party. This was an army. She thought of her father and her older brother, Jack, clearing stumps from the new pasture. "Prepare to be beaten tonight when we play checkers," Jack had said that morning. "I let you win last night, but tonight you will see who the real champion is."

"You didn't let me win," she had bristled. Jack had grinned to show he was teasing and hurried to catch up with their father, who was already heading for the pasture.

Their mother had chuckled as she cleaned up the breakfast dishes. "You two and your checkers games." Thinking of her mother made Hannah choke back a sob. It was washing day, and Hannah should have been helping. However, her mother had unexpectedly sent her to pick berries that morning. Hannah knew her mother was being kind, giving her a few hours of freedom from the never-ending work on their small isolated farm in western New York. "I have a taste for a blackberry cobbler," she had said with a smile when she woke Hannah.

A sudden crackle of gunfire sounded not far from the cave, and Hannah sank to her knees in despair. Why hadn't she tried to warn them? Wasn't it better to die with her family than to cower alone in this tiny cave? A small part of Hannah's mind admitted the truth. She did not want to die. She could not have outrun the quick-footed warriors. And even if she had made it back to her parents and brother, what chance would they have had against so many? No, if she had not remembered the little cave she and Jack had found when they were younger, she would be dead already. Or worse. The Iroquois often tortured their enemies. That was what Mr. Van der Beck, their nearest neighbor, had told Hannah's father when he came to warn him a few weeks earlier.

"There are rumors some farms to the north have been raided," he'd said, looking out over the peaceful valley. "I'm taking my family to safety, as are most of our neighbors."

Hannah's father shook his head. "I can't believe Englishmen would incite the Indians against their own people. At any rate, we have had no problem with the Indians."

"Some of the tribes are helping the patriots," Mr. Van der Beck said, "but they say the Iroquois have joined with the British. King George has promised to stop the westward expansion into Iroquois land. My brother brought a newspaper from Boston. It says that after George Washington drove the British from that city last year, most of the Tories abandoned their homes out of fear and went with the British to Halifax. Almost half the

people in Boston have left. Those who favor England are bound to be bitter."

"Thank you for the warning," her father had said, "but Boston is far away. I've seen no signs of trouble here. I'll not be driven from my land by a rumor."

And rumor it had seemed. Over a month had passed since that conversation, and nothing had marred the peace. Even Hannah's mother, raised in Boston and never comfortable living so far from her neighbors, had begun to relax.

The gunshots in the distance stopped suddenly. Hannah thought she heard a scream. She thought it might be Jack, but it did not seem quite human. She covered her ears and quietly sobbed.

It was nightfall before the screaming stopped. Still she did not move. She had seen the enemy arriving that morning in swift, silent birch-bark canoes. The canoes were beached along the muddy banks of the river, just a few hundred feet away. She could not venture out until the murderous savages had finished their cruel work and paddled back north again.

Her body was cramped and sore from the hard cold ground. She rubbed her arms through the rough material of Jack's shirt that she wore. She almost smiled when she thought of her mother's reaction to seeing her in her brother's clothes.

"Hannah Pritchard! What is that you are wearing?" Mother straightened her back and gestured with the long pole she used to stir the huge boiling kettle of clothes she was washing.

Hannah had paused, flashing her mother her brightest smile. "Jack's clothes are so much more comfortable, Mother. Remember how upset you were the last time I picked berries and tore my dress on some brambles?"

"It's not seemly for a girl of fourteen to be wearing britches," Mother had answered, shaking her finger and frowning. "Your father will not want to see you that way." She did not order Hannah to change, however.

"I think girls ought to be allowed to wear pants," Hannah said. Ignoring her mother's shocked look, she rushed on. "Think how much more comfortable it would be while we are doing chores. If I could wear pants, I could be helping Father and Jack."

"That's men's work," her mother said with a shake of her head. "Your place is helping me so you can learn how to run your own home someday."

Hannah sighed. "I wish I could do something first. Have an adventure. Have you ever noticed that whatever work women do is always waiting to be done again? You will just have to wash those clothes again next month. Dinner will have to be cooked again tomorrow. When Father and Jack are done today, the field will be done."

Her mother had chuckled as she used the pole to put Father's pants in a second big kettle to rinse. "You have such funny notions, Hannah, I ought to make you change."

"You are washing my dress," Hannah had pointed out. "My old dress is so small it is even more unseemly than Jack's clothes."

Mother had nodded. "I can't let it out any more. You have been growing faster than the weeds in my garden. I think there is a dress in my trunk we could make over for you."

Hannah had hugged her. "No one will see me," she said. "I will be back before Father and Jack return from clearing the pasture. And I will change as soon as I return."

Mother had smiled, shaking her head. "See that you do. And keep a watchful eye."

Hannah had glanced around at the peaceful farm. Near the house was Mother's large garden. It was late summer, and the beans and corn were nearly ready to pick. A small fenced pasture and barn were home to the oxen, Max and Tug, and Blossom the milk cow. Several chickens pecked for bugs about the yard.

Father had cleared more than twenty acres when they had first come here several years ago. Now that Jack was fifteen and old enough to do a man's work, Father had decided to clear another twenty acres. From where she had stood, Hannah could see them hard at work. Last winter, her father and Jack had cut down all the trees. Some they had split for firewood, but the rest, with the help of the oxen, they were dragging to a pile for burning. Max and Tug could pull up the smaller stumps, but her father would leave the larger ones and plant the wheat around them. Before he did that, however, Hannah and her mother would help by digging out rocks and piling them to be made into a fence.

"I'll be careful," she had promised her mother as she picked up the berry buckets.

The cool night air creeping into the cave was filled with smoke. Hannah sniffed in alarm. She crawled to the cave entrance and peered out. The moon was hidden behind the low hanging clouds, but a faint red glow was visible through the trees. What if the fire spread and she was trapped here in the cave? Then, as if in answer to her question, she felt the first few drops of rain. She crawled back to her corner.

Hannah's stomach growled with hunger. She groped around, searching for the spilled berries. When she found a few and placed them on her tongue, she nearly gagged. How could she think of food when her whole family was dead or dying? She forced herself to swallow a few, then curled on the ground, waiting for the night to pass.

In spite of the chilly night air and her hard stone bed, Hannah dozed fitfully, awaking just before dawn when the

invaders returned. The men made no attempt to be stealthy this time. They talked among themselves, and once someone laughed. Hannah felt her grief change to anger as she saw the flashes of British red.

A shadow hid the rising sun. Someone was just outside the cave. Had she survived all this terrible night just to be found now? She shrank back, shaking in terror.

An Iroquois warrior squatted in front of the cave and moved aside Hannah's camouflage. He stared at her silently. A scream tried to leap from her throat, but in spite of his ferocious appearance, something in his eyes made her stay silent.

His head was shaven, except for the long center lock. He wore nothing but a loincloth and soft moccasins. Intricate designs had been painted on his face and chest. In one strong hand, he gripped a war hammer, which was decorated with beads and feathers.

He continued to look at her and slowly shook his head. Then he stood, carefully replacing the bush. Hannah heard him say something to his companions in his own language.

For a long time, she did not dare move. What had happened? Was it possible that a savage like that was sick of the slaughter and had shown her mercy? How strange that the mercy had come from an Iroquois and not one of her own people.

She waited a long time to make sure they were all gone. The sun was high in the sky before she at last dared to leave the cave. Crouching low, she slipped through the trees to the place where she had first seen the canoes. They were gone, and only the smashed reeds at the water's edge gave signs that they had been any more than a dream. She turned and started the trek back to the farm, dread filling every part of her.

In the forest, no birdsong came from the trees. Not even the chirping of late summer insects filled the air. The acrid smell of smoke burned her nose. She trudged through the stubble of the burned cornfield. The barn was gone, burned cleanly to the ground, but part of the house had been spared by the rain. The clothes fluttered from the rope her father had strung for drying. Her brown dress was there, streaked with wet black ash.

She found her mother where she had fallen, near the kettle of rinse water. There was an arrow in her throat. Hannah wondered if she had even had time to scream. She stared at her mother's body dully, her mind unable to process it, too numb even to cry. Blood soaked the earth, and flies buzzed around the wound. She brushed them away, but they returned almost instantly. After several minutes, she pulled herself away. She had to find her father and Jack.

They were not in the field, although Max and Tug were there, their bodies still attached to the yoke. She searched for hours, but she did not find the rest of her family in the surrounding forest. Hannah allowed herself a faint hope. Perhaps they had somehow escaped. Maybe they had been taken captive. Indians did not always kill captives, she knew. Sometimes a boy like Jack was even adopted into the tribe.

She stood still, remembering the screams she'd heard, and suddenly she knew where they were. She forced her feet back to the barn. It was still smoldering in spite of the rain. With a stick, she poked through the rubble. She found Blossom first, though little was left of her. Father and Jack were not far away, their bodies black and twisted.

Hannah stumbled away from the barn. Her stomach cramped, and bitter bile filled her throat. The retching reminded her that except for the few berries she had nibbled in the cave, she had not eaten in almost two days. Although it filled her with shame to be thinking of food when her entire family lay dead just a few feet away, she rummaged through the trampled vegetable garden. She found only a few beans for her effort, and she made herself eat them.

She was so numb with horror that it was hard to think. She knew that the first thing she had to do was bury her family, but she could not imagine how she would manage that task. Her gaze returned to her mother's garden. The earth would be softer there. Near the smoldering debris of the barn, she finally found a shovel. The handle was burned, but it was still usable, and she set to work.

Under the first few inches of soil, the ground was hard. The day was hot, and sweat trickled down Hannah's head, making her eyes burn. She worked steadily, but hunger, heat, and grief made the progress slow. When the sun set, she was still not done. At last, she put down the shovel, noticing for the first time that her hands were blistered. She pulled up a bucket of water from the well, plunged her hands into the cool water, and splashed it on her face. Then she pulled her clothes from the line and put them on. She rolled up Jack's clothes into a neat bundle. Using it for a pillow, she curled up on the ground near a still-standing corner of the house.

In spite of her exhaustion, she lay awake for a long time listening to the night noises. An owl hooted, and she sat up, listening intently. Was it really an owl, or was that a signal between cruel-faced men slipping through the forest on moccasined feet? She had never been alone before. Always there had been Mother, Father, and even Jack to depend on. She knew she had to make some sort of plan to survive, but right now she was too weak and sick at heart to move. She closed her eyes and slept.

It was a nightmarish, fitful sleep, and when she awoke at dawn, she was still exhausted. Without opening her eyes, she felt the sun on her face. Slowly, she became aware of a drumming sound in the hard earth. She sat up quickly. Horses! Someone was coming. They must have realized that she had survived and come back to kill her. Fresh terror filled her as she scrambled to her feet frantically looking for a place to hide. Not enough remained of the house to shield her. Her only hope was to reach the forest and try to hide herself among the brambles.

Holding her skirts, she pounded through the burned cornfield, stumbling over clumps of incinerated stalks. There was a pain in her side, and her knees were scraped where she had fallen. She knew they would overtake her before she made it to the trees, but she raced on. Her breath came in ragged gasps that made her throat ache, and there were bright spots in front of her eyes. She heard shouting behind her. She willed herself to go even faster, but her body would not obey. A blanket of darkness covered her as she fell, unconscious, to the ground.

chapter two

The Road to Boston

Mr. Van der Beck patted Hannah. "You poor child." After Hannah had regained consciousness, he had half carried her to the shade of the remaining shell of the house. The grief she had held in all day had been released in a torrent of tears at the sight of a friendly face. Mr. Van der Beck poured water from a canteen on a rag and gently wiped her swollen eyes. Her sobs had ended, but her breath still came in ragged short gasps. Mr. Van der Beck glanced over to where the six militiamen were finishing the burial of her family.

"I finally convinced the militia in Albany to spare some men. We found all of the farms burned, but most of the people had already left."

He offered her a piece of dried beef from his pack, and Hannah gnawed on it listlessly. The militiamen finished their grim task and stood nearby, listening as Mr. Van der

Beck gently questioned her about the attack. The men did not look like Hannah imagined soldiers would appear. None of them wore uniforms. One of them did not look much older than Jack, and two were old enough to be grandfathers. One was a black man. Hannah stared at him curiously. Although her mother had told her there were black slaves in Boston, she had never seen a black man before.

As Hannah told her neighbor about the unexpected mercy from the Indian who had seen her in the cave, Mr. Van der Beck listened intently. He then said, "That may have been Joseph Brant. He is one of the leaders of the Mohawk. He is an educated man and a sachem for his tribe. Even though he has thrown in his lot with the English, there have been stories of his mercy."

"He didn't show any mercy to my family," Hannah said, her voice choking

Mr. Van der Beck looked at the freshly covered graves. "No," he agreed softly. "Do you have any family left?"

Hannah hesitated. "My grandmother lives in Boston. A traveler brought a letter from her almost a year ago. She wanted us to come back. I have not seen her since I was a small child. She did not approve of my father, and my mother said Grandmother was angry when we moved here. She thought it was too dangerous. I guess she was right after all," she added bitterly.

Mr. Van der Beck said, "Your father was a brave and stubborn man. That's what it takes to settle a new country. And that's what it will take to win this war."

After conferring with the soldiers, Mr. Van der Beck said, "It is too dangerous to stay here, and the men have to get back to Albany. I left my family there, too. You can come back with me, or I will help you get to Boston if that is what you want. There is no more we can do here."

Hannah leaped to her feet. "You are not going after them?"

"By your own account, there were about fifty men," Mr. Van der Beck said. "We are only seven."

"I could help," Hannah sobbed. "I can shoot as well as a man."

Mr. Van der Beck just looked at her. "Your family will be avenged. But not now. And not by us."

She knew he was right. She also knew the marauders were long gone. Still, she burned with anger.

The black militiaman had fashioned a crude cross and placed it over the grave. Another militiaman said a prayer. Hannah stood beside the grave, tearless now, a coldness creeping over her heart.

"We should go while we still have daylight," Mr. Van der Beck said. "Have you decided what you would do?"

Although Mr. Van der Beck looked tired and grim, his face was kind. She had seen his wife only a few times, but she remembered her as a sour-faced woman with a shrill voice. They had five small children, the oldest not yet eight. They didn't need another mouth to feed, although Hannah imagined she could be of help. She could scarcely picture her grandmother, but she did remember a gentle woman with soft hands. She recalled a town with big buildings and churches with tall steeples. And she fondly remembered the ocean—the smell of it, and the tall ships, sails billowing in the wind.

"I think I should go to my grandmother's," she said after a minute.

Mr. Van der Beck nodded. "A good choice, I think. A family should stay together."

Hannah looked around the place that had been her home for almost as long as she could remember. She wondered if she would ever see it again. Suddenly consumed with guilt, she took a last look at the graves. Why had she survived when her family had not? She thought of Jack's teasing, her mother's gentle smile, her father, stern yet kind. She choked back a sob. She picked up the bundle of Jack's clothes and walked slowly to the horses. "Wait," she cried, suddenly remembering. Running to a small bush by the remains of the house, she knelt and began digging in the dry hard dirt, first with her bare hands and then, failing, with a stick. At last, she was rewarded for her efforts. While Mr. Van der Beck watched in astonishment, she withdrew a small leather satchel buried in the dirt. "My mother hid this when she heard news of the war," Hannah explained.

Mr. Van der Beck stared as she held out the bag. "There are two silver buckles, four silver spoons, and a few coins. Mr. Paul Revere made them. Mother said he is the finest silversmith in the country. It will help pay you for taking me to my grandmother's."

Mr. Van der Beck glanced nervously at the militiamen. They, however, were some distance away with the horses and did not seem to be paying attention. "Put it away, child. You may need it later. I do not want to be paid for doing my duty as a neighbor. I am sure your father would have done the same for my family." He watched as she rolled the treasures inside her brother's clothes. "Be careful not to let anyone see that you have that," he warned.

Hannah rode behind Mr. Van der Beck. When they reached the road to Albany, he and Hannah thanked the men for their help and started alone on the road to Boston. Since they had to share one horse, they were forced to stop often so the animal could rest.

Near the village of Pittsfield, a farmer offered a wagon and a fresh horse when he heard Hannah's story. Mr. Van der Beck left his own horse there until he returned.

Hannah settled gratefully onto the wagon seat. It was more comfortable, but just barely. In some spots, the road was fairly smooth. In other places, it was pitted with ruts, occasionally so deep that logs had been fitted across the span. The horse pranced gingerly over the logs. "At least the weather is dry," Mr. Van der Beck said. "In rainy weather, this stretch of road is almost impassable."

Hannah's thoughts were a jumble of confusion. Her grief was so overwhelming that it was almost painful. At times, she hated the British; at other times, she was angry with her own father for being too stubborn to heed the warnings. Over everything was the guilt. Why had she not tried to warn her family? Maybe she could have outrun the warriors after all. Jack would have tried. He would not have cowered in a cave, saving himself. Then the thoughts of Jack—his friendly teasing, the championship checkers game they had planned for that evening—would throw her into despair again. If only there was some way she could avenge her family. Then, at least, her living would have some purpose. But how would a girl get revenge on the whole British and Tory armies?

Hannah and Mr. Van der Beck stopped one night at an inn. As they ate dinner, they listened to the news from other travelers. The talk was about the war and little else. At first, the war had gone badly, but last year George Washington had driven the British from Boston. In a daring move last Christmas, he had sneaked his troops across the Delaware River at night. He had surprised the Hessian mercenaries and driven them out of Trenton, New Jersey. Later, the Americans had won a battle at Princeton, also in New Jersey. Suddenly the thought of winning the war against the powerful English army did not seem so impossible.

Mr. Van der Beck slept in a room with six other men. The innkeeper's wife took a candle and led Hannah to a smaller room upstairs. There were three cots with thin straw mattresses. A large woman, who was snoring loudly, already occupied one of the cots. Hannah stretched out on another cot and covered herself with the thin quilt. She slept fitfully. The quilt had a sour odor, and the mattress was itchy. She rose with the first light. Her arms and legs itched, and when she looked at the quilt in the daylight, she could see tiny black fleas jumping about.

At every stop along the way, Mr. Van der Beck inquired for someone who would take Hannah the rest of the way. At last, in a village not far from Boston, they met a man taking a load of produce into Boston to sell, and he agreed to deliver Hannah to the city. Hannah bid a tearful good-bye to her kind companion, wondering if she had made a mistake not to have made her home with him.

"Can you read?" Mr. Van der Beck asked suddenly.

"Some," Hannah said proudly. "My mother taught me. Father thought it was a waste of time for a girl, but Mother convinced him that then I could read the Bible."

"Good," Mr. Van der Beck said. He handed her an envelope. "This is a letter to my sister. She owns an inn in Portsmouth, New Hampshire. If for any reason, your grandmother does not treat you kindly, or you do not find her, I have asked my sister to give you a job. It will be hard work, but you are used to that. She is a good woman. She will treat you well."

"Thank you," Hannah said, hugging him. "Please let me pay you."

"You just did," he answered with a smile. "Now go," he said, waving to the wagon where Mr. Massey, the farmer, was waiting.

Mr. Massey was not as pleasant a traveling companion as Mr. Van der Beck had been. He was a short, dark-haired man with deep wrinkles and a constant frown. He hardly glanced at Hannah and seldom spoke. The wagon was piled high with cabbages and, occasionally, when they went over a bump, one would roll out. Mr. Massey would then stop and, with a grunt, let Hannah know she was to run back and fetch it. Then, without a word, they would be off again.

Mr. Massey was missing most of his teeth, but between the few remaining ones, he kept a tight grip on a long-stemmed pipe, which he constantly puffed. The foul smell of tobacco mixed with the pungent odor of cabbages made Hannah feel sick. She found herself dreaming of her grandmother's house. Maybe Grandmother would take her to the wharf to look at the ships. She remembered doing that when she was little and wishing she could sail in one across the sea. She wondered if Grandmother would be shocked at her appearance. Her dress was stained, and she had not bathed in weeks. In addition, she had fleabites, and she itched terribly.

When they stopped for the night, Hannah counted out the last of her coins for a dinner of boiled pork and potatoes. It was bland but filling. Because she was not sure when her next meal might be, Hannah forced herself to eat until she felt stuffed. She had nothing left but the spoons and buckles, and she had no idea of their worth if she was forced to use them for barter. Fortunately, by midmorning, a city came into view.

"Boston," Mr. Massey grunted.

Hannah's impression of Boston was that it was a town of steeples. It seemed like almost every building had one. A tall hill overlooked the town, with a tower built on the top. "That's Beacon Hill," Mr. Massey explained. "In times of danger, the beacon was to be lit to warn the town. I haven't heard that it has ever been used, though."

As interesting as the town was, the waterfront fascinated Hannah even more. Tall masted ships crowded the harbor. The area swarmed with people. Swarthy dangerous-looking sailors loaded barrels of molasses, bundles of cotton, and other goods on and off the wooden wharves. Businessmen inspected goods and shouted orders. Coarse-looking women with bright red lips and false-looking smiles strolled by, flirting with the sailors.

"Looks like two ships managed to slip by the British," Mr. Massey said. "Last month, our privateers captured a British ship loaded with blankets and warm clothing for the British troops. Wait until the redcoats spend a winter in New York in their summer underwear." Mr. Massey chuckled in a rare show of good humor. He looked at Hannah. "This is no place for a young lady," he said firmly, although Hannah would have liked to stay and watch all the activity.

He drove his wagon to a large brick building. There were other wagons arriving with supplies. Women with baskets were inspecting vegetables and sniffing at fish to see if they were as fresh as the vendors claimed.

Mr. Massey was obviously taking her no further, so after thanking him and receiving a grunt in reply, she retrieved her bundle and started down the busy street. Houses hugged the narrow street, many with shops on the first floor. Some of the older ones had second floors that actually hung over the streets. The sights and sounds were dizzying, so unlike the quiet life she had known on the farm. Wagons and carriages rumbled down the narrow cobblestone streets, forcing her several times to press up against a building to keep from being run down. In one carriage, two girls in beautiful dresses and bonnets looked disdainfully at her as they passed. Hannah rubbed at her face with her sleeve, knowing they had probably mistaken her for one of the street urchins she saw begging for a few pence at every corner. She saw one snatch an apple from a cart. The driver cursed and flipped his whip, catching the boy on his back. However, the boy hung on to his prize and disappeared down another street.

Two gentlemen passed by. "Can you direct me to Wood Lane?" she asked timidly.

"Get away," one man said roughly, pushing her so that she almost fell. The second man gave her a pitying look. "That way," he said, pointing. "It is close to the North Square."

Hannah stumbled down the street, trying to step over the worst of the filth. She had to stop several times more to ask directions, but finally she found a small wooden sign announcing Wood Lane. The houses along this street were large and imposing, many of them brick. She stood for a minute, unsure of what to do now. She had no idea which one was her grandmother's.

A black woman hurried by carrying several baskets heavy with food. "Do you know which house belongs to the Widow Payne?" Hannah asked.

"That one," she said, pointing and at the same time giving Hannah a pitying look before she hurried away.

Hannah wondered at the look. Did she look so terrible that even a slave pitied her? She rubbed again at her face and tried to straighten her hair. She was sure the first thing her grandmother would do would be to draw her a bath. Perhaps she would even have a clean dress that would fit her. And food. Hannah suddenly realized how hungry she was. She raised the knocker and tapped boldly.

A tired-looking woman holding a baby opened the door. Behind her, Hannah could see children, a whole house full of them, it seemed. Several of the younger ones crowded around their mother and peeked at Hannah.

"Oh, I am sorry," Hannah exclaimed. "I must have come to the wrong house. Someone told me this house belonged to the Widow Payne."

"It did," the woman said. "She left with the British Army and the rest of her kind."

"Her kind?" Hannah willed herself not to crumple to the ground in despair.

"Loyalists," the woman spat out the word as if it was poison. "Everyone in town was forced to open their homes to the British. The Widow Payne, however, did so

willingly. She even entertained General Gage, the British commander, at dinner parties in his honor. She's lucky she wasn't tarred and feathered." She peered suspiciously at Hannah. "Why are you looking for a Tory like her?"

"She is my grandmother," Hannah answered. "I didn't know."

Before she could finish, the woman interrupted. "Don't go thinking you can put any claim on this house. The city confiscated all the Loyalist property. We bought this house fair and square." With that, she stepped back inside and firmly shut the door behind her.

chapter three

Alone

Clutching her bundle tightly to her chest, Hannah plodded down the street. Her mind was numb with despair. Where should she go? Why hadn't she gone with Mr. Van der Beck? Now she was alone, with no family and no friends to help her. Maybe she had no choice other than to become like the other orphans she had seen running wild through the streets. Between the houses she could see the harbor and the white sails of the ships billowing in the breeze. How lovely it would be, she thought, just to sail away from all her troubles.

Furiously wiping her eyes, she sat down with a sigh on some wooden steps leading to a shop displaying fabrics in the window. She hated this city and its unfriendly people and noise. From where she sat, she could see the harbor with its long wharves, but it only served to remind her of how far away she was from her home and how very much she had lost. She thought of her mother's gentle ways, how after supper she read to them from the Bible, the only book they owned. Her father would be busy, perhaps making a chair or mending the yoke for Max and Tug. Father did not know how to read, but he was proud that his wife could. "That sounded fine," he would say when she closed the book. "I could listen all night." Hannah and Jack would smile at the look of love that passed between them.

Hannah choked back her anger. It was the British and Tories who had brought the Indians to end their peaceful life. To learn that her own grandmother was one of them was almost more than she could bear.

She got up and walked aimlessly along the harbor road. She was tired and hungry. Soon it would be night, and she had nowhere to stay. She felt the weight of the silver in her pack. If she could find somewhere to sell the buckles and spoons, perhaps she could find her way back to Albany. Mr. Van der Beck had acted like they might be valuable. Who could she find in this town to give her a fair price?

A large poster in the window of a large brick inn caught her eye, and she stopped to read it. "Portsmouth Flying Stagecoach," it proclaimed in large letters. As she read more, her excitement grew. She reached into her bundle and looked at the envelope Mr. Van der Beck had given her. She was right. Portsmouth was where Mr. Van der Beck's sister lived. She looked again at the poster. The

cost was thirteen shillings and six pence, and the stagecoach left every Friday morning from Charlestown, stopping at inns along the way. If she could find somewhere to sell her silver, maybe she could get enough for the fare.

She tried to remember which direction she should go to walk back to the marketplace where Mr. Massey had taken her to that morning. Surely she could sell the silver there. Maybe Mr. Massey was still there and could advise her. Although he was surly by nature, she thought he might be honest enough. She walked briskly in what she hoped was the right direction. Now that she had a purpose, she walked quickly. She almost missed the small sign in front of another store.

"Paul Revere, Silversmith," she read. She almost smiled with relief. Maybe he would buy back his wares. At least he could tell her how much they were worth. Feeling hopeful, she pushed open the door and stepped inside.

The gleaming pieces of silver displayed on the tables made her gasp with pleasure. Beautifully shaped spoons, tea sets, bowls, pots, and boxes were neatly arranged on tables and shelves. In an open back room, she could see several apprentices hard at work. A red-haired boy sat at a table polishing. Several others were pounding bars of silver with heavy anvils. One of them rushed into the display room and confronted her. "Go on, get out of here," he scolded. "This is no place for the likes of you."

Hannah faced him defiantly. "I would like to see Mr. Revere."

"Mr. Revere is an important man. He doesn't have time for your kind."

"I have business with him," she said boldly.

The boy laughed out loud. "What possible business could you have with Mr. Revere?"

Hannah untied her pack and unwrapped the buckles and spoons. "These were made by Mr. Revere himself. I wanted him to tell me what they are worth."

The boy suddenly came around the counter and grabbed her arm. "Who did you steal these from?" he said roughly. Still holding her, he called to the red-haired boy. "Henry, go and find a constable." Her accuser tried to wrestle the treasures from her grip, but Hannah would not let them go. "No! They are mine!" she screamed.

Henry hesitated, but the first boy shouted at him. "Go. Hurry."

Henry dashed out of the door just as a well-dressed man entered. He was a plump, still handsome man of about forty. The apprentices froze, and from the respectful look on their faces, Hannah knew this must be Mr. Revere himself.

The apprentice, who was still holding Hannah's arm, spoke first. "This girl has stolen some silver pieces. I've sent for the constable."

"I did not steal them. They are mine." She tried to wrench herself loose so she could face the silversmith.

Mr. Revere stared at her. "Why, you are only a child," he said "How could you be the owner of this silver?"

The silversmith listened intently while Hannah explained. When she had finished, he said, "I knew your grandmother. She was a good customer in past years. When the trouble started, she chose to remain loyal to King George." He gave her an understanding look. "Don't judge her too harshly. She was an elegant lady, too set in her beliefs to change." Mr. Revere turned to his apprentice. "Turn her loose. Then go tell the constable he will not be needed after all." He looked at Hannah again. "Have you a place to go?"

"I thought I would go to Portsmouth," Hannah said. She showed him the letter. "I need to sell the buckles for the fare."

"I will give you two pounds for them. That will be enough for your fare and some to put aside for a start in Portsmouth." Ignoring her gasp at such a fortune, he handed a pound note to Henry, who had just returned from his search for the constable. "Take this to The Sign of the Lighthouse, where Mr. Stayers has his headquarters, and buy this young lady a ticket on Friday's stage. See that you bring back the change."

The apprentice nodded and ran back out of the shop. "Now, you come with me," he said to Hannah. "Tomorrow is Friday. You will stay at my house tonight. In the morning, I will have my apprentices row you to Charlestown. The stage leaves from there at six in the morning."

His kindness brought tears to her eyes. Only a few hours ago, she had been thinking about how unkind the people in this city were. "I don't want to be a bother," she said meekly.

Mr. Revere smiled. "You have had enough hardship for anyone so young, I expect. I have a daughter about your age. Her name is Sarah."

When the apprentice returned, Mr. Revere walked with Hannah to his home. The house was large, with three stories and three huge fireplaces. Every room, it seemed, was full of children. In a basket by his mother was the newest one, a baby named Joseph. Mrs. Revere took one look at Hannah and ordered Sarah and Frances to fetch a large tub.

"Yes, Rachel," answered Sarah. Hannah was surprised that Sarah had used the woman's first name.

In no time at all, Hannah was soaking luxuriously in hot, steamy, rose-scented water. Sarah and two younger

sisters chatted comfortably while they helped Hannah wash her hair.

"Rachel is our stepmother," Sarah volunteered, answering Hannah's unspoken question. "Our mother died when I was ten. Rachel is nice, though."

"The British brought Indians to murder my family," Hannah told her.

Sarah looked sympathetic. "Yes, Rachel told us. It must have been frightful, living so far away from civilization. Although," she added darkly, "it wasn't much fun here either. The British soldiers were everywhere, and they stopped you on the street to ask what you were doing."

"They stopped the ferry, too," Frances, a girl of about ten, remarked. "Father had to get someone to row him across when he went to warn Mr. Adams and Mr. Hancock that the British were coming to arrest them."

"They arrested him and took his horse," said a solemn girl named Mary, who looked about eight or nine years old. "Mother Rebecca was very worried."

"I threw your dress away," Mrs. Revere said as she bustled in with towels. She laid out a pretty blue dress. "There isn't enough time to make you a dress, but I think this will fit you."

The next day, Hannah, clean, rested, and well fed, said good-bye to her new friends. Mrs. Revere gave her a small satchel to carry her bundle. "There is a change of clothes for you." Mrs. Revere said giving her a hug.

Hannah had to scurry at a good pace to keep up with her benefactor as he walked briskly down the city streets. Although the sun was barely up, carts and horses clattered down the cobblestone streets as the city came alive. The sun had not yet burned away the mist hanging over the water and the town, giving the morning a ghostly chill. Henry and the apprentice who had thought she was a thief were waiting by a small rowboat. Hannah climbed into the boat and sat down. When she turned to thank Mr. Revere, he was already walking quickly toward his shop.

chapter four

Portsmouth Flying Stagecoach

The advertisement had promised a "convenient and genteel" way of traveling, but five minutes into the journey Hannah wondered if she had made a terrible mistake. There were six passengers in the small coach. A man and his wife sat across from her, and next to them sat a man with a badly pock-marked face in rough clothing that reeked of onions. Hannah had hoped to get a seat by a window, but she was crowded between a very plump lady—who introduced herself immediately as "Opal Jones from Concord"—and an older woman in a severe black dress, whose elbow poked Hannah every time the coach went over a bump.

The rocking motion of the coach mixed with the smell of onions made Hannah's stomach churn. Still, it was exciting to be dashing along at breakneck speed.

The coach rattled and creaked over the bumpy road as the horses' hooves thundered away the miles. "Oh," the fat lady moaned. "What if we tip over?"

Hannah felt alarmed, but the young husband noticed her pale face and said reassuringly. "That hardly ever happens, and when it does usually no one is hurt."

"It feels like the motion of a ship," the onion-smelling man observed.

"You have been on a ship?" the young wife asked. "I saw them in the harbor. It seems like it would be lovely to sail on one."

"I've been on plenty," the onion man answered. "I am a ship's carpenter by trade. I am traveling to Portsmouth to join a crew. I can tell you that a short sail you would find pleasant, but a long voyage is dull. Unless you run into a storm."

"Or pirates," the lady with the sharp elbow spoke for the first time. She looked at Hannah. "I was not older than you when our ship was attacked by Calico Jack and his female companions."

"Female?" The young wife looked pale.

"It's true. They dressed in men's clothing. Anne Bonny and Mary Read were their names. Not long after we were ransomed, they were caught in Jamaica."

"What happened to them?" Hannah asked curiously.

The old woman shook her head. "I never heard. There are not very many pirates left nowadays," the old woman said. "Most of them were captured and hanged. There was even one hanged in Boston harbor."

"The new government is giving letters of marque to ship captains, allowing them to attack British ships as privateers," the seaman said. "They can keep part of the booty, if they share with the government."

The young husband was a newly ordained minister, and his wife's face glowed with pride as she explained he was going to be an assistant pastor at a large church in Providence, Rhode Island. The minister was fiercely patriotic. He told them that he had been in the crowd listening to the first reading of the Declaration of Independence.

The conversation was so lively that Hannah forgot how uncomfortable she was. It was a surprise when the stage stopped for a change of horses. There was just time enough to eat a quick lunch set out by the tavern owner before they were off again.

That evening, after a plain but hearty meal at yet another tavern, Hannah was exhausted. She was grateful when the innkeeper showed them to their rooms.

After a hasty breakfast the next morning, they climbed again into the crowded coach. The horses stamped their feet impatiently, while the driver accepted several packages to deliver from the townspeople and secured them with the rest of the luggage. Then with a crack of the whip, they were off again. There was much talk about the war. Everyone agreed that it was time to be free from the whims of a king far across the ocean, who really did not understand the colonies. Hannah told them her story. When she talked about Mr. Revere, the young minister interrupted.

"Why, he is quite famous, you know." No sooner had these words left his mouth than there was a loud crack. The stage seemed to leap into the air. Hannah had a brief glance of the driver, flying by the open window in the door with a startled look on his face. Suddenly the stage lurched sideways. For a second it teetered, as though it would stay upright. Then it began to tip, almost in slow motion. Opal Jones screamed as they fell in a tangle of bodies and luggage.

The stage skidded a few feet, then stopped. For a second, it was quiet. Then the passengers began to moan and mumble, and the sailor cursed. Hannah had ended up on the bottom of the pile of upset passengers, the wind knocked out of her by Opal, who had managed to end up on top. "Oh, my," she moaned. "I knew this would happen."

By now, the driver had recovered from his tumble. He managed to open the door, now facing straight up.

He gave a hand to Opal. Inside the coach, the sailor and the young husband pushed until the driver managed to drag her out of the cabin, and he helped her slide down to the ground. One by one, the other passengers climbed out and stood, somewhat shaky but intact, by the side of the road.

The driver soothed the horses, still attached to the stage with their eyes rolling white in fear. Then he inspected the stage. "No great harm done," he announced. "Lucky that axle didn't break, or we would have had to stay here until someone fetched a carpenter from the next town."

The coachman told the passengers to line up next to the tipped stage. Everyone obeyed except Opal Jones, who was still moaning about her bruises. Hannah thought peevishly that she probably had more bruises than Opal. After all, she had been underneath. She did not say anything, however, even when several other passengers grumbled. "When I say three, everyone push," the driver ordered. "One, two, three."

With a mighty effort, the coach was righted. It bounced several times on the springs and then was still. "There," shouted the driver, "good as new."

In short order, the luggage was stowed and the passengers climbed in. They were off again, although at a more sedate pace.

Opal Jones left them at the next small town, still moaning about her injuries. She told them that word had come to her that her mother was quite ill, and she was going to care for her. Hannah was glad no one had said anything to her, and she left with everyone's well wishes. However, with only five in the coach, the rest of the journey was more comfortable.

When they arrived at Portsmouth, Hannah was delighted with the looks of the town, smaller than Boston but snuggled around a harbor that was almost as big. She saw several shipyards, and the warehouses beside the docks looked busy and prosperous.

"It must be wonderful to sail on such a ship," she said to the ship's carpenter.

The sailor grinned, showing his missing teeth. "The sea gets in your blood. Too bad you are not a lad. I could get you work as a cabin boy or cook's helper."

"They hire boys my age?" Hannah questioned.

"Aye," he said cheerfully. "I started as a cabin boy when I was but twelve."

"Do you know where you are going?" the young minister asked Hannah as they said good-bye.

"It is an inn called the Red Rooster," Hannah replied. "Mr. Revere thought it wasn't far from the stage stop."

"It is on Queen Street," said the old lady in black, giving her directions

Hannah said good-bye. Clutching tightly to her satchel, she trudged down the street, trying to swallow her nervousness. What if Mr. Van der Beck's sister did not need help? Or even worse, what if she was not even there? Hannah had a little money, but it would not last long without a job. Her mouth was dry with nervousness, and she was exhausted from the journey. So much had happened in the last few weeks. She wished for a quiet room where she could rest and collect her thoughts.

She found the inn easily enough. It was a large three-story house. The whitewashed walls were turning gray from the sea air, but the window boxes were filled with brightly colored flowers and a bright red rooster was painted on the sign. Taking a deep breath, Hannah pushed open the door and walked in.

Nearly every table was filled. A dark-haired woman cleared dishes from heavy wooden tables and carried platters of delicious-smelling food from the kitchen. She brought two pitchers of ale and walked through the room filling tankards and chatting with the customers. Through the kitchen door, Hannah could see a thin black woman stirring pots in a huge fireplace. Her long skirts were gathered up and tucked into the waist of an apron so that a scandalous amount of leg was showing. Hannah smiled. She had seen her mother do the same thing. Long skirts could easily catch fire, and everyone knew at least one woman who had died from the burns.

The woman with the ale pitchers suddenly noticed Hannah. A surprised look passed over her round face. Then she smiled and walked over to Hannah. "Are you hungry, child?" she asked.

"Are you Mr. Van der Beck's sister?" Hannah asked shyly. She fumbled in her pack and handed the letter to the woman "He said to give you this."

The woman read the note. "Hallelujah!" she exclaimed loudly. "You could not have come at a better time. My girl ran off this morning. Madeline and I are buried in work." As she spoke, she almost pushed Hannah toward the kitchen. Grabbing a huge apron, she tied it around Hannah, talking all the while. "I am Lottie, and this is Madeline," she said cheerfully. "We will get better acquainted when our guests have gone."

"Take those plates before they get cold," Madeline said sharply. Lottie picked them up and hurried back to the dining room. Hannah hesitated, somewhat in shock. Madeline wiped sweat from her brow with her apron. She pointed to a table stacked with dishes and pots and pans. "Wash those," she said. "Be careful with the plates. They will break, and Lottie paid a king's ransom for them."

Hannah was surprised that a slave would speak so boldly and call her mistress by her first name. Hannah's mother had been against slavery and had told her that most slaves were treated harshly.

Madeline set two large tubs on another table. From the fireplace, she brought a large kettle of boiling water and divided it between the tubs. Hannah scraped the plates into a large bucket and, with a bar of soft soap, carefully scrubbed the plates. She had never seen dishes like these and did not have to be reminded to handle them carefully. In her own house, they had eaten from wooden plates her father had carved.

She worked quickly. Madeline said little, but from time to time, she gave Hannah a look of approval. The cooking smells made Hannah weak with hunger, but there was no time to rest. Lottie bustled back and forth, delivering food and bringing more dishes to wash. She gave Hannah's arm a gentle squeeze. "You are doing a wonderful job," she murmured.

Finally, business slowed. The clean dishes were stacked in a huge cupboard, and the last of the huge kettles had been scrubbed.

Lottie poured three glasses of ale and sat down at one of the tables in the now empty dining room. Madeline filled three plates with a delicious-smelling stew. Again, Hannah was surprised when Madeline sat down at the table with them.

"You are a hard worker," Lottie said.

"Thank you, ma'am," Hannah said.

"No 'ma'am' around here." Lottie laughed. "Just call me Lottie." Over bites of stew, Lottie questioned her. Hannah told Lottie about her parents and explained how Mr. Van der Beck had helped her.

Madeline shook her head sadly. "You've had a hard time, but you will be safe here. Everyone is worried about the British attacking Portsmouth, but we hear they are farther north."

"I wish I was a boy," Hannah burst out. "Then I could join our army and fight them."

The women were silent for a minute. "That would not bring them back," Lottie said gently.

"Fighting is best left to the menfolk," Madeline remarked.

Hannah looked from Lottie to Madeline, wondering at their easy manner with each other. As if sensing her question, Lottie said, "Madeline is not a slave. She is a free woman."

Hannah smiled. She was relieved to hear that. The thought of Lottie's keeping a slave had made Hannah feel squeamish. She tried to smother a yawn.

"Oh, my. You must be exhausted. Come, I will show you where to sleep."

A narrow staircase ran up from the back of the kitchen. Taking a candle, Lottie climbed the stairs. "There are rooms to let on the second floor," she said. "You get there from the staircase off the dining room. This staircase is just for us," she explained as she climbed.

There were three rooms on the top floor. One was for Madeline, and one for Lottie. The third room was small but clean and had a narrow bed, small chest, a table, and a ladder-back chair. On the table was a metal bowl painted with flowers on the edge and a pitcher of water. "The necessary is out back," she explained. "But there is a chamber pot under the bed."

"The room is lovely," Hannah said.

"I hope you will be happy here," Lottie said. She set the candle on the table. At the door, she turned. "Do you like the ocean?"

"Oh yes," said Hannah.

Lottie chuckled. "Wait until you see the view from your window in the morning," she said as she softly closed the door.

chapter five

The Red Rooster

The first rays of sun streaming through the thin calico curtains awoke Hannah early the next morning. Remembering Lottie's words, she ran to the window and pulled back the curtains. "Oh!" she gasped. She pushed up the sash and leaned on her elbows, breathing in the salty air. From the third floor advantage, she could see far across the harbor. White-capped waves broke the gray-blue of the water. The ocean seemed to go on forever, finally meeting the sky in the distant horizon. Looking down, she could see a small garden with brightly blooming flowers surrounding a small table and two chairs. Madeline sat at the table drinking a cup of tea. She looked up and saw Hannah. "This is my favorite time of day," she called up.

"It is so beautiful!" Hannah called back. "I remember seeing the ocean from my grandmother's house. I think I loved it even then."

Madeline picked up her cup. "There is not much time for gazing at the ocean around here. Time to go to work."

The next weeks flew by. There was endless work to be done every day to keep the inn running smoothly. Hannah's days were filled with washing linens, sweeping rooms, and scrubbing dishes and pans. The women were kind to her, but they worked even harder and there was little time to rest. At night, when Hannah at last crawled into bed, she was almost grateful for her weariness. If she did not fall asleep at once, she thought of her family. She could not shake the feeling of guilt that she had hidden and not died with her family. If she could only seek some kind of revenge, perhaps there would be a purpose in surviving. Yet, there seemed little that a girl could do.

Each morning when she awoke, she looked out across the harbor. The sight of ships, sails unfurled, heading for distant shores filled her with longing. How exciting it must be to feel the wind pushing you to strange and exotic lands.

One night, Lottie seemed flustered as she refilled the pitcher of ale. She nervously patted a stray curl in place. Madeline cackled, "Oh, your fancy man must be about."

Hannah looked up from the pan she was scouring. "Who?" she asked.

"Captain Jones." Madeline chuckled. "He has all the ladies atwitter, even our Lottie."

"Don't be ridiculous," Lottie huffed. "I'm too old to be atwitter over anyone."

Madeline laughed again. "See that you remember that."

Hannah peeked into the common room. Captain Jones was a short man, not much taller than she was, but he was handsome and spoke with a Scottish burr. He was dressed grandly in his uniform of the new Continental Navy and carried a sword at his side. He was accompanied by a lady.

"His name is John Paul Jones," Madeline whispered behind her. "There are rumors that is not his real name. I heard that he changed it because he killed a man in a fight. He is waiting while they finish building his new ship. It is called the *Ranger*. Every time he comes, he has a different lady on his arm."

The next day was Sunday, and the inn was closed. After church services, Lottie insisted they take a day of rest. They washed their hair using rainwater saved in a barrel, and they each enjoyed a long soaking bath. "Some people think too much bathing is bad for you," Lottie said. "I think people would smell much better if they did." Hannah loved the rose water Lottie added to her bath, and with her first wages, she bought a bottle of her own. After their baths, they made themselves a light supper and talked for hours.

Hannah learned that Lottie was a widow, and her husband had left her the inn. Madeline had come from a land far away. Madeline's eyes clouded with pain as she told her story. The slave traders had caught her when she was just a girl and had gone to the well for water. "The slavers killed my father and the boy I hoped to marry one day. I don't know what happened to my mother. I was chained in the hold of a ship. It was dark, and there were rats. People got sick, and the smell was so bad you could scarcely breathe. Every few days we were taken, a few at a time, to the deck. The sailors threw buckets of water over us as if we were animals."

"Oh, Madeline," Hannah said softly.

Madeline shook her head and went on with her story. "I was fortunate and was not sold to the plantations in the South. A man and his wife in Boston bought me. They treated me kindly and even taught me to read and write. I became a good cook, and my owners sometimes lent me to their friends to cook for parties. They allowed me to keep what I earned, and I saved it. After seven years, I bought my freedom, and I came here."

Hannah's eyes filled with tears as she listened to her new friend's story, but Madeline patted her hand. "I have a good life," she said cheerfully. "A person must take what life hands them. You, no doubt, would have married a farmer and never seen the ocean. Yet I can see that you are drawn to the water."

It was true. Every Wednesday morning, Lottie insisted Hannah take the morning off. Sometimes Hannah wandered through town glancing at all the shops. Mostly, though, she was drawn to the seaside. She watched men unload the ships. Merchants arrived with wagons to take huge bundles of cotton, sugar, and coffee to the many warehouses along the road.

One morning, she wandered through one of the many shipyards along the shore. She found a large rock and perched on it, watching the workers. She could see Captain Jones's new ship the *Ranger*. It was painted black, with a band of yellow, and its three masts were rigged with square sails. Hannah thought it looked every inch like a fighting ship, a perfect match for its dashing captain. Rumors had been flying at the inn about a disagreement between the builder and Captain Jones. It had delayed the sailing for several months.

Hearing footsteps along the rocky shore, Hannah turned to see Captain Jones himself approaching. "Good morning, miss," he said. Squinting closer, he said, "You are the kitchen girl at the Red Rooster."

Hannah nodded. "I like to come here on my free morning."

Captain Jones motioned to several ship carpenters who were staring at Hannah. "It is not safe for a young girl alone here."

"No one has bothered me," Hannah answered. "Is your ship nearly ready to sail?"

"I had hoped to be gone by now," he said. "It is difficult to assemble a crew. Everyone wants to join with the privateering ships. All they care about is sharing in the spoils. I shall sail to England and give them a taste of war on their own shore."

"I wish I could go with you," Hannah said. "I hate the British."

Captain Jones laughed out loud. Then seeing the look of anger on Hannah's face, he apologized. "I am sorry child. Miss Lottie told me a bit of your story. The idea of a young girl on a fighting ship is ridiculous, though. Allow me to strike a blow at the British for you."

When Hannah did not reply, he said, "If you were a boy you could be a cabin boy, or a powder monkey fetching the powder for the cannon."

"What does a cabin boy do?" Hannah asked.

Captain Jones shrugged. "Carries messages, cleans the captain's quarters, brings his meals, just makes himself useful."

"I could do all that," Hannah said.

Captain Jones shook his head. "I am not one of those who think that women are bad luck on a ship. Nevertheless, there is no place for a woman on a ship's crew." He got up and strode toward a small rowboat waiting to take him to his ship. Then he stopped and called back a warning, "Nor at the shipyards. It is dangerous here for a girl."

Hannah bristled with irritation as she walked back to the inn. If Jack had been here, Captain Jones would have let him sail. Yet she was almost as strong and, in fact, could do almost anything that he did. An idea was forming in the back of her mind, but she said nothing to Lottie and Madeline when she returned.

The next Wednesday, Hannah rose early. Taking Jack's clothes out of the trunk, she dressed quickly. She had grown some over the past few months, and the clothes, baggy before, now fit perfectly. She combed her hair straight and tied it back with a leather strap in the fashion worn by young men. Then she studied her reflection in the looking glass. Blushing, she suddenly realized that it was still obvious that she was a girl. She took off the shirt and bound her chest with several strips of cloth. This time, after putting her shirt back on, she was pleased with her reflection. With her thick brown hair pulled away from her face and her clear green eyes, she looked like any other boy running errands along the wharves. She went down the stairs to the kitchen.

Lottie sat at the old scarred desk where she did the bookkeeping, and Madeline was busy kneading the dough for the endless loaves of bread sold every day at the inn. Neither woman looked up. "You are off, then?" Lottie said finally. Her mouth fell open as she stared at Hannah. "You look like a boy."

"Everyone says it is not safe on the wharf for a girl," Hannah exclaimed.

"Humpf," Madeline snorted disapprovingly. "In years past, you would have spent time in the stocks, going out in public dressed like that."

Lottie's mouth had finally closed. "Maybe it is not such a bad idea. Who is to know but us? She certainly looks like a boy."

"Humpf," Madeline snorted again. She shook her head. "The minute she walks, people will know she's a girl."

Hannah pictured her brother's walk. There was a bit of swagger to it, an easy long-limbed gait, that celebrated his gender. She crossed the room, taking longer strides, trying to concentrate on freely swinging her legs and arms.

"Better," Madeline said, going back to her dough. "I still think it is a bad idea, but I suppose you will be safer."

No one gave her a second glance along the shore, and no one seemed to connect her with the hardworking girl at the Red Rooster. Occasionally, she was given an errand, for which she earned a penny. "Help me lift these bundles, boy," sailors unloading ships would call. Making her voice low, Hannah would tell them her name was Jack.

In her boy's apparel, she squatted close to the workers, listening for information about the war. She learned that the British kept prisoners of war locked on old derelict ships in harbors. Living in filth and fed little, many of the men died of starvation and disease. Listening to these stories made her desire for revenge even stronger.

One Wednesday, the wharf was buzzing with excitement. Large groups of people stood on one of the docks watching men unload a small two-masted ship. Hannah approached the group. Her curiosity won out over her reluctance to speak with strangers. "What is happening?" she asked.

A lady standing nearby was wearing an enormous hat adorned with feathers, bows, and what looked like a real stuffed bird. She pointed to the ship. "One of our privateer ships has returned with British treasures to sell."

The cargo was laid out along the cobblestone road. Nearly everyone in town, it seemed, had come to shop among the treasures. Hannah stared at the privateers. Some were heading straight for the taverns' grog shops. Others hugged their wives and children, who had gathered on the shore. They did not seem different from any of the others.

With a guilty start, Hannah remembered Lottie and Madeline. They would want to look over the goods for sale. She hurried back to tell them about the ship.

Seeing their excitement, she offered to stay and watch the inn. With repeated reminders to mind the loaves

already browning in the ovens, the two women grabbed their shopping baskets and hurried away.

Hannah dashed up the stairs and changed out of Jack's clothes, then rushed back down to the kitchen. It was warm and sticky in the kitchen, and the smell of fresh bread made her hungry. Two of the loaves were ready. Using a long-handled paddle, she removed them from the brick oven at one side of the fireplace and set them on a table to cool. Rain was beginning to fall, but the two women had not returned. Hannah sighed, suddenly lonely. She missed her family, Jack's teasing, and her mother's gentle chatter as she prepared the noon meal with Hannah's help. Hannah wiped furiously at her eyes. Lottie and Madeline were kind to her. Still, when she thought of her life stretching ahead, filled with the never-ending work of running the inn, she felt like a prisoner.

She took a broom and swept the dining room, straightening tables and chairs. A paper was crumpled in one corner. She smoothed it out and started to read it just as the two women, dripping wet and shopping baskets full, burst in the door. Hannah hastily folded the paper and hid it in the pocket of her apron.

chapter six

Privateer!

Soon after the last guest had gone, Hannah said she had a headache and hurried to her room. The women had been excited about their purchases when they returned that morning, but there had been no time to lay them out and admire them. Hannah knew they had bought several pieces of fine glassware that had belonged to a British captain. And they had returned with packages of sugar, tea, and spices like cinnamon, nutmeg, and ginger. Hannah had seen a length of beautiful rose-colored silk, and she knew the women wanted to share their treasures with her over their evening glass of ale.

That Hannah had a headache concerned Lottie and Madeline, and they shooed her off to bed, which made Hannah feel guilty. Still, she could not wait another minute to read the advertisement she had found. Setting the candle down, she retrieved the paper from her pocket and

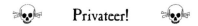

smoothed it out on the table. "An invitation to all brave men who want to serve their country and make their fortune," she read. The name of the ship was *Sea Hawk*, and Captain James Nelson was signing a crew to fight the British. He promised that each man would have a share in the booty, depending on his position. Skimming through the list, she discovered that cabin boys received only one half a share.

Hannah sat on the narrow bed. Was she brave enough to do it? Everyone said being on a ship was hard work. Still, she doubted it was harder than the work she did at the inn. The thought of leaving Lottie and Madeline made a hollow pain inside, but the thought of her father and Jack, tortured and burned in the barn, filled her with resolve. She might never have another chance at revenge.

She read the notice again. Interested men and boys were to report to the wharf at dawn one week from this day.

Hannah spent a sleepless night tossing and turning, unable to make a decision. When she dragged herself out of bed the next morning, there were dark circles under her eyes and her head really did hurt.

"Oh, child, are you getting sick?" Lottie brushed her head softly, feeling for a fever.

She sounded so kind and worried that Hannah jerked away, her guilt making the movement seem more abrupt than she planned. "I'm fine," she said, trying to sound cheerful but failing.

Lottie gave her a startled look, but she said nothing more. She checked the morning market list and put on her hat and cape. The weather had been getting cooler, and a brisk cold wind swirled loose papers and leaves across the street. Usually, she invited Hannah to go with her, but this morning she did not.

Hannah had seen a look pass between the two women, the raised eyebrow and the slight shake of head. They were acting as though they were her mothers, she thought, upset at the idea. They were always fussing about and watching her. The next moment, she was ashamed of her thoughts. Both women had been far kinder than any kitchen worker had a right to expect. Hannah knew they both did care for her almost like a daughter.

"If something is troubling you, it might help to talk about it," Madeline said, giving her a sharp look.

Hannah shook her head. "Nothing troubles me. I just didn't sleep well last night."

Madeline nodded, but did not speak.

"Didn't you ever wish you could take revenge on those slavers that captured you?"

Madeline put down the knife she was using to cut vegetables. "Perhaps when I was young. There was no way to do it, though."

"But what if you had the chance? Would you have taken it? And what if it meant leaving the people who were kind to you?"

Madeline stared at her. "What are you planning, child?"

"N-nothing," Hannah stammered. "I was just wondering."

"The people who bought me did not do so to protest slavery. They wanted a slave. That they were kind to me is commendable, but if there were no one to buy slaves, the slavers would have no business. They were as guilty as the slavers. Yet when the smallpox took them a few years ago, I grieved."

"I wouldn't grieve to see any of the redcoats die. Or the Tories!" she added hotly. "There is a small part of me that can understand the Indians hating us, but the British and Tories kill us because we want to govern ourselves."

"Your grandmother is a Tory," Madeline reminded her.

Hannah shook her head. Her voice was bitter. "She is lost to me."

Madeline shrugged. "You must do what you must do. Think carefully, though. Revenge will not bring back your family."

The next few days passed all too quickly. Though she did not completely admit it to herself, Hannah had made up her mind to go. She did not share this decision with

Lottie and Madeline, for fear they would do something to stop her. Still, although outwardly everything remained the same, they seemed to sense she was leaving. She often caught Lottie looking at her with a sad expression that she would quickly cover with a big smile.

In her room at night, Hannah sewed an extra pair of britches and a shirt, using the old ones as a pattern. She rolled the clothes in a bundle with her few possessions, reluctantly leaving the bottle of rose water behind.

On the last morning, she slipped out of bed before dawn. Leaving a note on the kitchen table, she hurried through the silent streets to the wharf. In spite of the early hour, the area was noisy and alive with excitement. Workers loaded last minute supplies on the ship, and another group of men clustered around a table set on the rocky beach.

"Is this where you sign on for the *Sea Hawk*?" Hannah asked, making sure her voice sounded boyish.

The man she spoke to clapped her on the back so hard she almost staggered and fell. "Ho! Here's a fine young lad wants to be a privateer." He shoved her to the front of the line.

The captain looked up from his papers and gave her a hard stare. "You are young," he said flatly.

"I'm fourteen," Hannah said. "I can work hard. And I can cook."

"And what do your parents think of you putting out to sea?" he asked.

"I'm an orphan," Hannah said.

The captain leaned back in his chair and studied her. "You are small."

"But I am strong," Hannah said desperately. "And maybe I will grow."

This brought hoots of laughter from the men behind her. Hannah felt her ears grow red with embarrassment, but one of the men spoke up. "Give the lad a chance, Captain. I've seen him hanging around the docks, always ready to lend a hand for a penny or two."

"What do you think, Mr. Gaines?" For the first time, Hannah noticed a young well-dressed, handsome man standing nearby.

The man nodded. "We need a cabin boy. And Dobbs could use some help in the kitchen."

"What is your name, boy?" asked the captain.

"Jack, sir. Jack Pritchard."

"Make your mark here," the captain said, pointing to one of the papers.

"I can read and write, sir," Hannah said as she signed the paper.

The captain looked pleased. "You may be a good help to me. Welcome to the *Sea Hawk*, Jack Pritchard."

chapter seven

Setting Sail

Foul weather kept the *Sea Hawk* from sailing that morning as planned. The sailors settled in, grumbling about the delay, but Hannah was glad for the time to explore the ship. She questioned her decision repeatedly in her mind as she observed the sailors. Most of them seemed to be seasoned hands, although a few looked as lost as she felt.

It was not too late to change her mind, but she feared the captain's anger if she were to reveal that she was a girl. She reminded herself to walk like a boy as she followed the first mate down one of the hatches to a small partitioned room, scarcely bigger than a cupboard next to the galley. "You will bunk here. That way you are close by when you are needed," Mr. Gaines explained.

In spite of the blustery weather, Mr. Gaines called for all hands to assemble on the deck. On a curved deck above them, Captain Nelson stood looking every inch a captain, Hannah thought. "Men," he said, "as soon as there is a break in the weather, we will set sail. Those of you who have sailed before know what is expected of you. Those few landlubbers, I expect you to learn your duties quickly. I run a tight ship. If you are on deck, you are working. The only exception is a half an hour at sundown and Sunday. The *Sea Hawk* was built to be a merchant ship, with a normal crew of about fifteen men. We have a crew of forty. That means lighter duties, but it also means we have less room. I will not tolerate drunkenness on my ship. Each man may have a pint of grog with each meal, and an extra one on Sunday."

Next Mr. Gaines introduced himself. "I am the first mate. You will take your orders from me. Obey those orders quickly and thoroughly, and you will find me a fair master. Disobey and you will pay a severe price."

Captain Nelson spoke again. "We all have our reasons for being here. The British will call us pirates. But we are privateers in the service of our new country. The *Sea Hawk* is a fast ship. With a little luck, you will come back from this voyage richer men. Our purpose is to deprive the English of supplies and help supply our own army. We are privateers, yes, but we are also a ship of war."

With that, he turned and walked back to his cabin. Mr. Gaines spoke to several seamen, assigning the first watch.

Then he motioned to Hannah. "You will carry messages for the captain," Mr. Gaines told her. "The captain likes his tea as soon as he rises. You will serve the officers their meals. And you will be responsible for keeping the captain's quarters tidy." He showed her pens of chicken and ducks on the main deck, and another with two goats. "These animals will also be in your keeping," he said. "They must be fed and watered and the manure washed off the deck each day. Can you milk?"

Hannah nodded. "Yes, sir."

"Good. That, too, will be your duty. You will take the milk to the galley and help cook. Do your duties well, and the captain will treat you fairly. Shirk your duties, and you will feel the whip."

"I'll do my best," Hannah said solemnly.

"Sir," Mr. Gaines reminded her.

"Sorry, sir," Hannah replied.

"Very well," Mr. Gaines said. "You may take this time to become familiar with the ship, and then introduce yourself to Mr. Dobbs. The captain has ordered the men to remain on the ship so he can leave at the first break in the weather. Even though we are at port, they still have to eat."

"Sir?" Hannah said as the first mate turned to go. "Where is the necessary?"

Mr. Gaines laughed. "On a ship it is called a head. He pointed to two doors on the bow of the ship. "On some ships, it's right out in the open, but the captain had Mr. Bowden, the carpenter, built partitions. The captain has his own off his cabin."

Hannah gave a sigh of relief not missed by Mr. Gaines. "Bashful, are you?"

Hannah shrugged, trying to look nonchalant. She could not explain that it had been one of her main concerns. With a door on the necessary—head, she corrected herself—it seemed that it would be possible to hide her identity. That she did not have to share the sleeping quarters with the rest of the crew had been welcome news, also.

The weather was dreadful. Howling winds drove the icy rain so that it stung her face and hands. The ship pitched and rolled against its moorings, and it was hard to keep her balance. She made her way to the door that Mr. Gaines had pointed out and discovered that it was a simple seat set out over the water. She could see the ocean swirling angrily below. She relieved herself quickly. She wondered about cleaning herself until she noticed a wheel with a rope. When she pulled on the rope, up came a cluster of feathers.

Outside the door, she heard cheerful whistling. "Did ye drown in there, lad?" boomed a voice. Trying not to think of how many men had used the feathers, she cleaned herself and left quickly.

"They call me Whistling Sam," said the first man waiting. He was probably only about twenty-five, but his skin was brown and leathery from years at sea, and it made him look older.

"I'm Jack," said Hannah, remembering to make her voice low.

"You best be covering those pens," Whistling Sam warned. "Captain won't take kindly to losing his meat supply."

Thanking him for the advice, Hannah hurried to the cages. One of the hands, an old man with no teeth to speak of, pointed to a roll of canvas near the cages. The man had deep wrinkles, and his ears stuck almost straight out. He wore a knitted cap, and when he took it off to scratch his head, Hannah saw that he was bald. His eyes were deep set and sparkled with good humor. He helped her cover the pens to protect the animals. Even in this weather, Hannah noticed that the old man wore no shoes. He grinned when he saw her glancing at his bare feet. "The decks get slippery. Bare feet have saved many a sailor from slipping over."

Hannah looked at the swirling black waters and shivered.

"They call me Ratso," the old man said. "Is this your first ship?"

"I'm Jack," Hannah said. "It is my first time at sea."

"You best learn your way around quickly," Ratso advised. "The back of the ship is called the stern. The captain's quarters, officer rooms, and dining room is there." He pointed. "That's where you will be mostly, I expect. Where the captain stood when he talked to us is the quarter deck."

Hannah thanked him and set off to explore the ship. The main deck had two tall masts. A sailor told her one was the main mast and the one closer to the stern was called the mizzenmast. On the main deck, she saw a pump and winches for the anchor. Several hatchways led below. It was easy to spot the galley hatch, because a large metal pipe protruded through the deck. Another hatch led to the gun deck. Hannah walked quickly by the huge guns chained to the deck.

She opened a door and found herself in the crew's quarters. Several men were playing cards, Their hammocks were tied back, but the room was cramped and damp. The carpenter had a small room to himself. His room was full of lumber and worktables, leaving barely enough space for his hammock. There were several storage rooms on this deck. One was full of extra sails and ropes. Below that was the hold. It was dark and had a terrible smell.

She hurried to the galley, glad that most of her time would be spent there. Mr. Dobbs was already hard at work. The galley was small but efficiently arranged. A brick stove and ovens took up one whole wall. A large bucket of sand sat nearby in case of fire. Along another wall were cupboards and shelves filled with dishes, pots and pans, and utensils. Several large worktables took up most of the remaining space.

Mr. Dobbs was about sixty, Hannah guessed. He was small, and, like many of the sailors, he had leathery and wrinkled skin. His long face seemed frozen in a grimace of displeasure.

"I suppose you know nothing about cooking," he said, eyeing Hannah.

In spite of his looks, his speech was of an educated man, and his voice was surprisingly gentle. Hannah thought she detected an amused twinkle. She almost thought they might become friendly.

"I do, sir," she said. "I worked at an inn."

He gave her another look. "Did you now? You may be of some use after all." He filled a teapot and set it on a tray with a cup and a biscuit and cheese. "No need for 'sir.' Just call me Dobbs. Take this to the captain. 'Tis rough out there. Mind yourself."

Hannah climbed back on the deck, carefully balancing the tray against the wild wind and spray from the water.

"It's Jack with your tea," Hannah called as she knocked.

Captain Nelson sat at his desk, frowning in concentration as he studied several charts unrolled before him. "Put it on the table, boy," he said absently. Hannah did so, furtively looking around the room. Where the rest of the ship seemed built for efficiency, the captain's quarters looked rich and comfortable. Large windows made the room airy and bright. There was a large bed covered with a colorful quilt, mahogany tables, chests, and a thickly woven Persian rug on the floor.

"Like it?" asked Captain Nelson, chuckling when Hannah blushed that he had caught her staring.

"Yes, sir. It is wonderful."

"The *Sea Hawk* was built to be a merchant ship. I planned to bring my wife on her first voyage. Instead, she waits in Boston." He waved a hand, dismissing her.

Hannah hurried back to the warmth of the kitchen. Even moored, the ship swayed and lurched alarmingly, and her stomach was uneasy. Still, the men had to be fed. Dobbs prepared two separate meals in the tiny galley. The officers had roasted chicken, turnips, and cabbage, and a custard for desert. The rest of the crew had a plainer meal of a stew made with salt pork, soaked to take out the salt, and biscuits that were so hard Hannah could hardly chew them even after soaking them in the stew. Still, the men fell eagerly to eating when Hannah delivered their meal.

By the time the pots were scrubbed and hung on their hooks, Hannah was exhausted. She had only picked at her own supper, so queasy was her stomach. Dobbs poured her a cup of tea and gave her a bit of custard left from the officers' meal. "You've done well today, lad." He hesitated a second before the "lad," and Hannah looked at him quickly to see if he suspected. His face, however, showed nothing, and he went on. "You are a good worker. Many of the boys who come to be cabin helpers are hiding from the law or are a worthless sort. You are different."

"I'm here to fight the British," Hannah said.

"Are you now? And what has a young lad like yourself got against the British?"

Hannah blurted out the story of her family's massacre, giving Jack a different name since she was now using it herself. Dobbs listened carefully, not saying anything until she was done. "I'm surprised you didn't run off to fight the Indians," he said finally.

"My father said we did not treat them fairly. He said that we sent blankets from people with smallpox and that it killed thousands of them. And one of them saved me. I hate Indians, but it is the British and Tories that brought them. We never did anything to the British except ask them for our freedom. And the Tories turned against their neighbors to side with them."

Dobbs drained his tea. "Go to bed now, lad. I'll be waking you early. I think the worst of the storm is over, so we should be on our way come light." He showed Hannah how to unroll the hammock from its hooks. He looked at Hannah's small bundle of possessions. "I'll ask the ship's carpenter to make you a chest. Most of the crew brought their own."

Hannah climbed in the hammock and wrapped the woolen blanket around her. The hammock swayed uncomfortably, and there was the sound of men's footsteps on the deck above. For a long time, she listened as the ship creaked and groaned in the wind and waves. She was sure she could never sleep. But no sooner than the thought entered her mind, she fell asleep.

chapter eight

Life at Sea

Even before Dobbs called loudly, "Wake up, boy. There's a crew to feed," Hannah was awake and sure she was dying. Her head ached. As soon as her feet touched the floor, she knew she was about to lose last night's dinner. She almost knocked over Dobbs, still standing by her door, in her haste to get on deck. His laughter followed her up the ladder. She crossed the deck and hung miserably over the rail, violently throwing up her dinner into the sea.

She realized that someone else was bent over the rail a short distance away. He straightened up and gave her a faint smile. "I see I'm not alone in my misery." He waved a hand weakly toward the empty horizon. "Do you suppose it is too late to swim back to nice solid land?"

"As soon as we die, they will throw us overboard and we can float back," Hannah said, trying to joke.

Their discomfort seemed to be a cause for much amusement to the men on the deck. Several sailors scrubbing the deck leaned on their mops, laughing at their misery. "What has Dobbs been feeding these young'ens?" one shouted.

"I don't know, but those two are going to have sharks following all the way to the West Indies looking for a snack!" shouted another with a loud guffaw.

Turning from the rail at last, but feeling no better, Hannah suddenly realized that the deck was a flurry of activity. The sails were unfurled and creaking against the masts, as the wind pushed the ship through waves that looked high enough to sweep everything overboard. Looking around, she saw no sign of land, only foam-capped waves in every direction. She hung tightly to the rail, as once again her stomach rebelled. This time, however, there was nothing left, and she was seized with dry heaves that wrung every bit of strength from her, and she moaned softly in misery.

The other seasick sailor had disappeared, but it was a few more minutes before Hannah dared leave the rail and stagger weakly back to the galley. "Sick or not, the work still has to be done," Dobbs said when he saw her.

"I'll try," Hannah said, swallowing hard.

"Eat a biscuit," he said. She shook her head. "Do it," he said more forcefully. Then, a bit softer, he added,

"They are too hard to chew. Soak it in some tea first. Seasickness is worse if your stomach is empty. You'll get your sea legs in a few days."

Dobbs showed her how to set the table in the officers' dining area using wooden storm trays that kept the plates from sliding across the table. Then, with her arms piled high, she climbed to the deck and ran straight into a stocky sailor with a long scar across his cheek that gave his face a permanent twisted leer. Hannah just barely managed to keep from falling and hold onto her burden, but the sailor let loose with a string of profanities that burned her ears, and he aimed a hard kick at her leg. With a cry of pain, Hannah stumbled back, dropping her load on the deck. The plates clattered and rolled on the hard deck and several broke.

"What is all this commotion?" Mr. Gaines stepped out of the officers' quarters.

"This orphan cur walked right into me, sir," the man with the scar said. He looked defiantly at several members of the crew who had paused in their work to watch. No one spoke up for Hannah.

Hannah rubbed her leg, which was already swelling. She opened her mouth to protest but noticed Ratso shaking his head, warning her to be silent.

"I'm sorry, sir. I didn't watch where I was going," Hannah said.

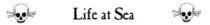

"Clean this up. Any more breakage will come out of your share," Mr. Gaines said sternly to Hannah. "And you, Mr. Larson, get back to your duties," he said shortly to the scarred man.

Furious, Hannah stood up and stacked the undamaged trays and dishes. Ratso watched Larson walk away, then bent down to help pick up the shards from the plates that had broken. "He's a mean one. Best not to cross him, or you'll find yourself at the bottom of the sea with your throat slit."

Hannah looked at him in horror, but he moved away without saying anything more.

"Here's two more plates," Dobbs said evenly from the stairs. Hannah wondered if he too had seen Larson's attack.

She took the plates and hobbled to the officers' quarters, arranging everything the way Dobbs had shown her. Then she limped back to fetch the captain's tea. When she stepped inside the galley door, the cooking smells made her stomach roll uneasily, and she ran back to the rail and retched again.

Dobbs handed her another biscuit, which was already softened. "Eat more," he said. He waited until she had choked down a few bites before handing her another wooden tray, this one with a steaming teapot and a cup. He handed her a small covered bowl full of sugar. "The captain likes a spoon of sugar in his tea."

Hannah went back again. She knocked at the captain's door and entered when he called out permission.

"Put it on that table," the captain said. "And pour me a cup."

Hannah stood shock still. The captain was shaving using a long razor—and he was completely naked.

Hannah was so flustered that she almost forgot to lower her voice. "Oh, I am sorry, sir," she stammered. "I thought you said to come in." She busied herself with the tea to avoid looking at him.

The captain chuckled when he noticed her red face. "I'm no different than you, lad, under my clothes. Nothing to be embarrassed about. "

"Oh, I am not, sir," Hannah said, thinking quickly as she measured out the spoonful of sugar. "I didn't want to embarrass you."

Still avoiding his eyes, she left his quarters and made her way back to the galley. The day passed in a blur of exhaustion. She served meals to Captain Nelson and Mr. Gaines. Mr. Hailey, the second mate, ate with them. He was a sharp-faced man who seldom spoke and appeared ill at ease around the captain.

After she cleared the dishes from the officers' breakfast, she went back to the captain's quarters. She

straightened the room and made the bed. Unlike the hammocks the men slept in, the captain had a real bed with a feather mattress. Instead of a rough blanket, his had soft linens and a quilt.

Next she carried heavy pots of oatmeal to the crew's quarters. When she had fetched everything back to the galley, it was time to scrub the breakfast dishes and pots.

Her ankle was throbbing. She was limping badly as she fed the animals. She felt sorry for the chickens. They would not survive this journey. They clucked softly as she threw them some extra grain. The two goats pushed up beside her, bleating loudly for attention. She milked them quickly, trying not to remember mornings at home when she had milked Blossom. Next she shoveled manure off the deck. Mr. Hailey showed her how to scrub the deck around the cages with sand and a sandstone bar. At least on her knees she did not have to stand on her sore ankle. When the deck was clean, she spread new straw and hobbled back to the galley for her own breakfast.

By evening, she was exhausted, and her ankle hurt so much she had to bite her lip to keep from crying out. "Let me see that ankle," Dobbs said. He had a small chest beside him. When he opened it, Hannah could see it was filled with bottles and strips of cloth. "I'm also the ship's doctor," Dobbs said when she hesitated.

The ankle was swollen and bruised. Dobbs told Hannah to sit with her foot in a bucket of icy seawater. After the first gasp of cold, it did seem to soothe it. Without comment, Dobbs put on some salve and wrapped it in one of the cloth bandages, "It will heal," he said. His voice was gruff, but his touch had been gentle.

Every morning, one of Hannah's chores was to go down in the hold for the wood used in the ovens. This was the task Hannah dreaded the most. The light from her lantern barely penetrated the inky darkness of the hold, and small rustlings told her there were rats. With one hand holding a lantern, she could carry only a few pieces of wood at a time. Most days, she had to descend into the bowels of the ship six times before Dobbs was satisfied. As soon as she was finished, Dobbs would cheerfully announce that it was time to start the midday meal.

It was barely light when her day started and nearly dark again when she was finally done with her duties. She noticed the ordinary seamen changed shifts every time the ship's bells rang. "They work four hours on and four off," Dobbs explained, "but that is round the clock. At least we can sleep through the night."

As soon as her chores were done in the evening, Hannah stumbled to her hammock. Her stomach was still rebelling, although she was not as sick as she had been. Her ankle was healing, too, but it was still swollen and

purple and made her walk with a limp. Hannah found it difficult to sleep in a hammock. She tossed and turned, trying to find a comfortable spot. She thought of her comfortable bed at home and remembered how she had sometimes complained at the endless chores. How foolish she had been! Even though the work was hard, there had always been time for fun.

Even the hard work at the inn had been eased by the kindness of Lottie and Madeline. Although she had not been at the inn very long, she was surprised at how much she missed them. Dobbs seldom spoke and smiled even less. There was no one on the ship to call her friend.

She wiped a tear from her eye, scolding herself for her weakness. She had chosen to join the ship, she reminded herself. There was a chance to extract some sort of revenge on the British, and if she was honest with herself, she had wanted the chance for adventure. With a sigh, she turned again. There was a thump, and two green eyes glowed at her. Something large and furry brushed against her. Screaming, she tumbled out of the hammock.

Soon Dobbs was there, holding up his candle. "What in tarnation is wrong with you, lad? You're screaming like some silly female."

"There was a rat in my bed," Hannah stuttered. "I felt it."

Dobbs laughed a deep belly laugh that made him bend over holding his sides. He held the candle up so Hannah could see. Perched in the corner, tail twitching at the disturbance, was the biggest orange cat Hannah had ever seen. "There's your rat, lad. That's George, the ship's cat." Dobbs laughed again. He started to shoo the cat away, but Hannah bent down and patted the cat on his head. A tremendous rumbling came from deep in his throat.

"Now, don't go making a pet of him," Dobbs admonished. "He has a job just like the rest of us. He's here to catch those rats you are so afraid of."

"I didn't know there was a cat on board," Hannah said with all the dignity she could muster.

Dobbs chuckled again. "Get some sleep," he said. At the door he turned. "You might want to bite your tongue the next time you feel the urge to scream. Crew hear you, they'll be calling you a girl."

George hopped back in the hammock as soon as Dobbs had gone. Hannah stroked the cat for a long time before she fell asleep. She thought about Dobbs's remark. Was he really trying to save her some teasing, or did he suspect she was a girl?

In the morning, she discovered that the weather had improved some, although it was still cold and rainy, and the seas were rough. The officers' quarters stayed dry, but waves washed over the decks and leaked down into the crew's quarters, making everything damp. And there was a terrible smell. "That's the bilge water," a young sailor, not much older than Hannah, explained when he saw her sniffing. "It collects in the bottom of the ship. The smell gets worse the longer we are at sea." He shrugged and grinned. "You'll get used to it." Hannah recognized him as the sailor who had been sick beside her. He helped her lift the heavy pots of salt pork and beans on the table. "My name is Daniel," he said, offering his hand.

"I'm Jack," Hannah said, shaking his hand.

"Mr. Bowden, the carpenter, has something for you," Daniel said.

Hannah went to Mr. Bowden's room and peeked in. The room smelled of sawdust, oil, and varnish. The carpenter was smoothing a piece of wood, but he looked up and pointed to a small chest. "Dobbs asked me to make it," he explained. "He said you didn't have a place to keep your belongings." He brushed off her thanks and returned to his task.

Pleased, Hannah carried the chest back up to her room and stowed her extra clothes in it.

By the end of the first week at sea, the ship's crew had settled into a smooth routine. Hannah's stomach still churned unpleasantly at times, and she still walked with a limp, but she was so busy she had little time to dwell on her misery. If Dobbs did not keep her occupied every moment of the day, Mr. Gaines found something for her to do.

Every morning, the decks were scrubbed. It took nearly two hours to do it properly, and often Hannah was assigned to that task in addition to the deck around the animal pens.

It was a constant strain to remember to walk like a boy and keep her voice low; sometimes Hannah thought that was more tiring than the work. Still, it seemed to be working. If anyone noticed her voice was sometimes high, they put it off to her young age.

In the short leisure time before bed, Whistling Sam started teaching her how to tie knots. "Every good sailor knows knot-tying," he explained, whistling softly as he worked.

"Why do you whistle all the time?" she asked one day.

He shrugged. "Most people whistle when they are happy. So when I hear myself whistle, I think I must be happy. Then I have to whistle."

Hannah was grateful that as the cabin boy she was not required to climb the ropes, although her new friend Daniel had offered to help her. Much of each sailor's day was spent climbing the ropes. When the wind was strong, Mr. Gaines ordered them to reef the sails. She watched Daniel and the other sailors tie the sails up with ropes. "That keeps them from tearing so much," Daniel explained. Even so, mending torn sails was a constant job, as was inspecting and repairing the ropes. On calmer days, the sails were unfurled to catch every bit of breeze.

One morning, she was scrubbing decks with Ratso. "Why do they call you Ratso?" she asked.

The old man laughed. "When I was a young man I could climb the ratlines better than anyone," he answered, "like your friend Daniel." Hannah watched Daniel scurry up the ropes to the top of the main mast far above them and intently search the horizon for signs of another ship.

"What happens if you fall?" It made her feel queasy just to watch.

"You die," Ratso said cheerfully. "Doesn't matter much if you hit the deck or the ocean." He shrugged. "It happens."

On Sunday, Mr. Gaines assigned only duties that were absolutely needed, and the men were allowed a day of rest. Dobbs led Hannah down in the hold and showed her two barrels. "That one has oranges, and the other apples," he said. "Captain Nelson read that fresh fruit might help prevent scurvy. Some people don't believe it, but the captain wants to test the idea. So every Sunday, each man will get an orange or apple with his rations."

"Make sure the lids are put back, and check now and then to make sure there's no bad ones to ruin the barrel." Hannah helped him count out the proper amount. She had never tasted an orange. She sniffed the fresh smell with delight.

"What is scurvy?" she asked.

"Just about the worst sickness you've ever seen. First you get weak and you get a rash. Then your teeth fall out and your gums rot. If you don't get to land, you die."

Hannah shuddered. "And an orange can stop it?"

Dobbs shrugged. "I don't know, but I guess it's worth a try."

They carried the oranges up to the galley. Dobbs showed her how to peel the skin and eat the juicy pieces. "Oh, they're wonderful!" she exclaimed.

"You go pass these out. Tell them it is captain's orders that they eat them," Dobbs said

They had sailed far enough south that the weather was getting warmer. In fact, it was almost uncomfortably humid, and the skies in the distance were dark. "There will be a storm later," Ratso predicted when she gave him his orange.

"I hope not," she said, remembering to make her voice boyish. "Daniel has promised a game of checkers."

Ratso peered at the distant clouds. "You best get started if you want to play on deck."

She glanced around for Daniel and saw that he had been assigned lookout duty. He gave her a wave from the top of the main mast high above her. Hannah hoped

the storm would hold off until Daniel's watch was over. It would be pleasant to sit on the deck and play.

Most of the men were lounging about the deck, smoking pipes, reading, or fishing. One man was playing a fiddle, and another was trying to follow along with a mouth organ. There were cheers at the sight of the golden fruit. It was a pleasant break from a steady diet of salt pork and potatoes or beans. Most of the men started peeling the treat immediately. She handed Larson his orange. He tucked it in his pocket, saying, "This will be a good trade for tobacco."

"It will keep you from getting sick," Hannah said. "Captain Nelson says you have to eat it."

Larson grabbed her by the collar and slammed her against the mast. "And who's going to tell him if I don't?" he snarled.

"No one is going to tell him anything," said Mr. Gaines, who had the uncanny ability to appear whenever there was trouble. "Because you are going to eat it right now."

Larson let loose of Hannah and glared at Mr. Gaines. For a few seconds, Hannah held her breath, thinking that he would defy the first mate. The rest of the crew were watching, too, suddenly silent.

Then Larson pulled the orange out of his pocket. "I was going to eat it all along, sir," he said sullenly. "I was just havin' a bit of fun with the lad." He started peeling the orange.

Mr. Gaines's hand was on the hilt of his sword. "Don't bother to peel it," he said with an icy voice. "Eat it all."

Larson stared, but something in Mr. Gaines's steely gaze made him back down. Slowly he choked down the orange, peel, pits, and all.

"I will convey your appreciation to Captain Nelson," Mr. Gaines said. There were several soft snickers from the men. Larson whirled around, but everyone was suddenly very busy minding his own business.

Hannah felt a chill that had nothing to do with the weather. Larson had been humiliated in front of his shipmates. He gave her a murderous look before he disappeared down the hatch.

"You've made an enemy," Ratso warned.

"Why does he hate me?" Hannah asked helplessly.

"He told some of the crew he planned on his nephew getting the cabin-boy job. That way he could get food from the officers' mess. The nephew was late to the docks, and you already had the job." The old man shrugged. "But men like that don't really need a reason."

From far above them, Daniel gave a shout. "Sail ho!"

Mr. Gaines replied instantly. "Can you see what it is?"

"It's a big one, flying the English flag. Looks like"—there was a pause while Daniel counted—"twenty-four guns. It's coming on us fast."

chapter nine

Storm

At Daniel's shout, all signs of a relaxing Sunday disappeared. Mr. Gaines shouted orders, and the crew jumped to obey. The captain, seldom seen in the last few days, paced the quarterdeck, watching the ship through his glass.

"Go below, boy. You'll just be in the way now," Mr. Dobbs said.

"What's happening?" Hannah gasped. "Are we going to fight?"

"We can't fight them. That's a warship. They could blow us out of the water, easy. We'll have to outrun them."

"Can we?" Hannah looked out at the English ship. Was it her imagination, or was it already closer?

Dobbs nodded grimly. "We can if we can stay ahead of them until the storm brings up a wind."

Every bit of sail was unfurled. Still, the warship stayed with them.

"Wet the sails, Mr. Gaines!" shouted the captain.

"Come on, Jack," Dobbs shouted. "We can help with that!"

Hannah was perplexed, but she leaped in to help. Some of the men positioned themselves on the ropes. Others tied buckets and lowered them over the side. They formed a chain to pass the buckets to the men on the ropes. Bucket by bucket, the men on the ropes wet down the sails and sent back the empty buckets to be refilled. Hannah's arms soon ached with the effort of lifting the heavy wooden buckets. Still she willed herself to keep up as bucket after bucket passed through her hands. When she finally had a chance to look, she noticed with satisfaction that they seemed to have widened the distance just a little after wetting the sails.

There was a flash of light followed by a terrific boom from the English ship.

The sailor at the wheel pulled hard to obey the order to turn hard to starboard, and the ship creaked nearly over on its side as the cannonball whizzed by, narrowly missing the ship.

For an instant, it seemed as though the *Sea Hawk* would continue to roll completely over. The men slid about the deck, and Hannah hung on desperately to keep from sliding off. Then, slowly the ship righted itself.

Now Hannah felt a breeze drying the sweat on her face. Although it was early afternoon, there was a strange yellowish cast to the sky, which began filling with low dark clouds. The sails flapped in the growing breeze, and the men cheered as the *Sea Hawk* gradually widened the distance between it and the British ship. Hannah saw that the seasoned sailors were watching the sky anxiously as the wind grew stronger. A few minutes before, they had needed every bit of sail, but now Mr. Gaines ordered men to climb up and reef in the sails, making them smaller.

She heard a low rumble of thunder in the distance, and the sky became so dark Hannah could barely make out the English ship, still doggedly pursuing them. She flinched as a jagged bolt of lightning raced across the dark clouds. The thunder was closer and so loud that the ship seemed to vibrate with the noise. Hannah was sick with fear, but she remained on deck, watching in fascination as the men prepared the little ship to fight the forces of nature.

A few minutes before, they had prayed for wind. Now, suddenly there was too much. The men on the ropes scurried to furl the topsails, their job made more dangerous by the howling wind. The English ship was forgotten for the moment as the sea swelled, and white-capped waves beat against the ship and splashed across the decks. Hannah suddenly remembered her responsibility to the animals. Although they were in a sheltered corner of the deck, they were at the mercy of the wind and waves.

Hannah fought her way across the wildly pitching deck to the frightened animals. She checked the ropes to be sure the cages were securely tied in place. Struggling against the wind, she fastened the canvas covers over the cages. The goats bleated pitifully, their eyes rolling in terror.

The waves grew higher, and the rain came down in cold hard drops driven by the howling wind. Her clothes were soon soaked and her fingers numb, but she managed to lash the canvas securely over the cages. Satisfied finally that the animals were as safe as she could make them, she turned to go below deck.

A sudden shout made her look up, but it took her a second to understand what she was seeing. A dark wall of water at least twenty feet high was sweeping toward her. She heard men screaming and cursing, but before she could move, the wave slammed over her. She gasped, and her mouth and nose filled with water. She lost her bearings as she was tossed about, but she knew she was being swept toward the rail. She was going to die. The idea surprised her more than it filled her with fear. For an instant, she gave into it. Then, suddenly, her body slammed into the bilge pump. She grasped for the handle, and at last her head was out of the water. She held on and gulped air into

her burning lungs. She heard a scream and saw a body drop from the ropes into the sea. Other men scurried to take the unfortunate sailor's place.

Then Dobbs was by her side. He pried her arms loose and practically pushed her down the hatch. "Get below," he shouted in her ear. "That's an order." He pushed the hatch door closed behind her to keep the ocean from flooding in.

Hannah huddled in the galley. She was cold, wet, and more frightened than she had been since that day in the cave. The ship rocked and groaned, and water poured in from small gaps in the deck.

She was not sure how long she had been there, when Dobbs came down. "The men will be hungry," he said matter-of-factly as he set about preparing a meal.

Hannah jumped up to help him. "Who was it that fell?" she asked.

"Jamison," Dobbs said, naming a man she knew only by sight. "Captain Nelson will have a service for him when this is over."

The men trickled down a few at a time, looking stunned, wet, and exhausted. With the ship still pitching wildly in the storm, it was impossible to cook, so they were given a slab of cold salt pork, a biscuit, and a tankard of ale. "Have we at least shook off the English devils?" Dobbs asked Whistling Sam.

"Blasted ship is still there. Mr. Gaines is hoping for a fog rising up after the storm. He thinks we can slip away during the night."

Daniel was in the next group to be fed. Hannah sighed with relief to see him, exhausted and soaked to the skin but still able to give her a tired grin.

"I feared that was you falling," Hannah said as she served him.

"Ha!" He laughed, giving her a friendly cuff on the arm. "Not until I have thoroughly trounced you at checkers."

"You had better get someone to give you some lessons then," Hannah joked back.

"That calls for a game to defend my honor. What do you say, Mr. Dobbs? Can you spare Jack for a while?"

Laughing, Dobbs threw up his hands. "In the middle of a storm? How are you going to keep the pieces on the board is what I want to know."

As if to prove his point, the bow of the ship lifted almost straight up and came down with such a mighty slap against the ocean that the whole ship seemed in danger of shaking apart. Pans flew out of the cupboards and clattered across the floor. The sailors could hear thumps and crashes all over the ship as every object not tied down slid into the walls. The men clung to whatever they could. Hannah was thrown violently to the floor. She thought of the heavy

ship's guns, wheeled but lashed tightly in place by ropes, and prayed they would not break loose. Hannah picked herself up, but no sooner had she done so, than another wave slammed into the ship, knocking her down again.

The men's faces were grim, thinking about their comrades still on deck. There had already been one man lost. How many more would be swept into the sea? For that matter, how much longer could the ship survive this punishment before it capsized and sank? No one spoke.

"I guess our match will have to wait," Daniel said.

The men laughed at that, the fear broken. "Wait until next Sunday when we all can watch," one man exclaimed.

"My money is on Jack," said another.

"No, Daniel," shouted a third.

Again and again the little ship was tossed by the waves, but after what seemed like forever to Hannah, the waves became smaller. The rain continued, but the sea grew calmer. The first watch was back on deck manning the pumps. The second group, including Daniel, were trying to sleep, although everything in the crew's quarters was soaked.

"I'd better check the animals," Hannah said. Dobbs nodded. "I hope we didn't lose any of them."

Fearing the worst, Hannah loosened the canvas covers she had fastened over the cages. One of the cages was missing. She found the frayed end of the broken rope, but the cage with its three fine laying hens had been lost. The other animals were wet and frightened, but alive. She talked to them calmly as she fed them.

"You have a way with animals," Daniel said, coming back on deck.

"I was raised on a farm, so I am accustomed to them," she answered.

"That's what I would like to do. We should take all our earnings and buy some land. We could be partners."

She shrugged, without answering, wondering what he would say if he knew that she was a girl. She thought he looked hurt, but he gave her his usual cheerful grin. "Well, think about it," he said as he went to find Mr. Gaines.

Just as Mr. Gaines had hoped, a light fog was forming. Hannah leaned on the rail. She could just barely make out the shape of the English ship.

Mr. Gaines sent Ratso and several other sailors up on the ropes. With pots of animal fat, they greased the ropes to help silence the creaking noise. "No lanterns," he ordered. "And no talking on deck. We will change course slightly and see if we can lose them."

Hannah went back below and crawled into her hammock. George came and hopped on top of her, purring as she scratched his ears. She lay for a long time, petting the cat and listening as the ship made its silent escape.

chapter ten

A Prize

"I'm glad we escaped," Hannah said the next morning as she prepared Captain Nelson's breakfast. "But when are we going to fight? Being a pirate doesn't seem much different than when I worked at the inn."

"Don't even let the captain hear you call yourself a pirate. He's a great patriot. He takes great pride that as a privateer he is helping the war." Dobbs looked stern.

"I'll wager the English think we are pirates," Hannah said.

Dobbs nodded. "I'm sure they do. If they catch us, we may not hang, because we are a ship of war. After a few months on one of their prison ships, we might wish they had, though."

"Then we won't let them catch us," Hannah said, pretending to fight with a sword.

Dobbs chuckled. "I never saw anyone so anxious to fight."

"It just seems like the English always outnumber us," she said. "We had to run away when my family was killed. And now we have run away again."

"I've sailed with Captain Nelson before. He likes to pick his battles. A wise man knows when to walk away from a fight." He chuckled again. "Or sail away, as the case may be."

Hannah measured out the tea leaves and poured water in the pot. "Have you always been a sailor?" she asked.

Dobbs nodded. "Since I was twelve. Started as a cabin boy like you. My father was a fairly prosperous businessman. My two older brothers were taken into the business. My father decided to apprentice me to a printer. I didn't like that idea much, so I ran off to sea."

"Do you ever see your family?" Hannah asked.

Dobbs shrugged. "Now and then. My brothers have grown rich and fat."

Hannah took the tray and hurried on deck. It was a cool morning, and the air was fresh, as if it had been scrubbed clean by the storm. The horizon was clear. She saw no sign of the English ship in any direction. Some of the crew were on deck, cleaning up under Mr. Gaines's ever-watchful eye. Daniel was among them. He nodded hello as he rolled up a long length of rope.

Larson was on deck, too. He was sitting down, mending sails that had torn in the wind. He pushed a long needle through the heavy material with a metal band he wore across his palm. When he noticed Hannah pause to watch for a second, he looked up and scowled.

"Good morning, Mr. Larson," Hannah said, trying to hide her fear of the man. He did not answer. As Hannah passed, however, he made a deep hawking noise and slowly and deliberately spat so that it splattered on Hannah's bare feet.

Hannah was so angry that her knuckles turned white where she gripped the tray. She bit back an angry reply and walked with the tray to the captain's quarters. She found him hunched over charts.

Captain Nelson looked up. "Put the tray there, Jack." He pointed to a table. Hannah did what he asked. Beside the table was a large open trunk. Hannah noticed with surprise that it seemed to be filled with ladies' dresses. Larson was still at his place when she returned. Hannah gave him a wide berth as she passed. He did not look up, but she heard him laugh softly to himself.

After breakfast, Captain Nelson called for all hands on deck. A sailcloth sack filled with rags lay near the rail. It was meant to symbolize Jamison's body, which could not be recovered during the storm. The men looked solemn as they gathered around the captain.

"Men," said Captain Nelson, "Mr. Jamison here was a hard worker. He died in the service of his country. His portion of our gain will be given to his widow."

One of the sailors sang a hymn in a surprisingly good voice, and then Captain Nelson said a few prayers. At the end of the short service, the sack representing Jamison's body was pushed over the side.

No sooner had it splashed into the sea than there was a shout from Ratso, high above on lookout. "Sail ho!"

There was a collective groan from the assembled men. Had the English warship found them after all that they had been through to escape? Then Ratso called out words that turned the groans to cheers: "Looks like a merchant ship. English. She is riding low. Looks like her holds are full."

The *Sea Hawk* was suddenly a beehive of activity. While Hannah watched in amazement, Captain Nelson ordered the course changed slightly so that they would cross the path of the other ship. An English flag was raised to trick them into thinking the *Sea Hawk* was one of their own. Hannah felt her excitement rising. At last, she would have some measure of revenge.

Mr. Gaines called sharply, "Jack! And you, Daniel! Report to Captain Nelson. Now!"

Hannah exchanged a puzzled look with Daniel. Ordinary seaman never dealt directly with the captain. Although waiting on Captain Nelson was part of Hannah's job, this did not seem like that kind of call. With some reluctance, they hurried to his quarters and knocked.

"Come in, boys," Captain Nelson called out.

"Have we done something wrong, sir?" Daniel asked, his voice trembling a little in spite of his brave front.

"No, no," said Captain Nelson. "I have a special job for you two." He looked up from his charts. "We want to reassure the ship that we are a merchant vessel just like they are. I need you two to do a bit of playacting to help. Are you up to it?"

"Yes, sir," they answered together.

"Good." Captain Nelson pointed to the chest Hannah had noticed earlier. "Pick an outfit."

Daniel pawed through the outfits. "These are women's clothes," he said in dismay.

"Exactly," Captain Nelson said. "Put them on. We want to convince the other ship's captain that we have lady passengers." He looked away from the charts again and smiled. "Look as feminine as you can."

Daniel was worried about the embarrassment of wearing women's clothing, but Hannah had an additional worry. It had been a constant fight to keep up the appearance of being a boy. She had to be constantly alert to keep her walk boyish and her voice low.

She did not want her crewmates thinking of her as a girl. She did not have to pretend her dismay as she looked through the trunk.

They slipped the dresses on over their own clothes, helping each other with the buttons. Daniel grumbled under his breath, which the captain pretended not to hear. Hannah looked at him. Even with a dress, she doubted that anyone would mistake him for a girl. He looked awkward in a gown of blue silk. The lace edging in the sleeves could not disguise large wrists and rough hands. Daniel looked completely miserable.

When they had dressed, the captain looked them over and nodded. "This mission may depend on you two," he said solemnly. "Just walk around the deck. Act like ladies. The other ship is bound to be watching through their glass. I want them to think you are ladies taking a turn around the deck."

The rest of the crew greeted them with catcalls and laughter when they went back on the main deck. Daniel fought to keep his good humor, although his fists were clenched.

Hannah put her hand on his arm. "Don't forget, the other ship may be watching. We have to act like ladies."

"There is a whole trunk full of dresses for the next man that laughs," Mr. Gaines said steadily. The other men fell silent instantly, although most still cracked smiles as they went about their chores.

"Let's make a good job of it," Hannah said. "Stroll by the rail where they can see us. Pretend we are enjoying the fresh air." She leaned in the rail, waving at the other ship.

At that very instant, a friendly face popped out of the water. It was a large creature, smooth and gray with a large snout. It seemed to balance on its tail, all the time making a strange clicking noise, almost like laughter. It seemed as though it was trying to talk. Then it suddenly dived into the water, bobbing up again a few feet away. Hannah saw that the whole ocean was full of these strange creatures. They swam along the ship almost like an escort, all the time keeping up their friendly chatter.

"They're dolphins," Mr. Gaines said from behind them. "They like to follow a ship along sometimes."

Hannah was delighted. She watched them, almost forgetting her mission. Even Daniel seemed intrigued.

The English ship was much closer now. Evidently, the ruse had worked, and the other ship had decided they were harmless.

"Gunners, to your stations," Mr. Gaines said, hardly raising his voice. "Quietly. No need to alarm them yet."

Several of the crew slipped down the hatch to the gun deck. At the same time, Mr. Hailey opened several chests and passed out muskets and pistols.

The other ship still had not realized their intentions. Hannah could see the captain, a portly man with a splendid bright red coat. "Where are you bound for?" asked Captain Nelson through a large speaking horn.

"I am Captain James Hamilton. My ship is the *Lady Jane* out of Barbados, headed for Halifax with a load of goods for His Majesty's army," the other captain replied.

"We are the *Sea Hawk*, American privateers," Captain Nelson shouted back. Haul down your sails or we will blast you out of the water." At that instant, the guns made their appearance through the ports, and heavily armed men on the *Sea Hawk* aimed their weapons at the other ship.

By now the ships were close enough for Hannah to see the other captain turn pale. Men on the *Sea Hawk* threw grappling hooks over the side and scrambled to the other ship. Hannah and Daniel tore off their dresses and ran to get weapons from Mr. Hailey.

"No need, lads," he said. "It's all over."

Daniel and Hannah watched as Captain Hamilton ordered his men to surrender and handed over the ship's manifest. Captain Nelson studied it with a pleased expression.

"Some privateers we are," Daniel grumbled. "Everyone else captures the ship while we stand around in dresses."

A Prize

"If it were not for you two we may not have gotten close enough to take them without a fight," Mr. Gaines said, overhearing Daniel. "You saved a lot of lives today. Theirs and ours. You can be proud of yourselves."

By now, more sturdy ladders and planks were in place, and some of the cargo was transferred to the *Sea Hawk*. After conferring with Captain Nelson, Mr. Gaines ordered Daniel and Larson to follow him to the other ship.

The men from the other ship, looking sullen and frightened, were herded onto the *Sea Hawk*. Each man was allowed to bring his personal chest. Hannah and Ratso were assigned to checking each one for weapons before the men were locked in a room below deck. Mr. Gaines posted two armed guards by the door.

"Jack, did you not tell me you can write?" asked Captain Nelson.

"Yes, sir," Hannah said.

"Come with me then, lad," Captain Nelson said. He led the way to the chart room and cleared off a table. "I will be sending the *Lady Jane* back to Portsmouth," he explained. "Men will want to send word to their families with the ship. I will send those who can't write to you."

Hannah nodded. "I can do that, sir."

"Good lad. The men will appreciate it."

For the next several hours, Hannah wrote for the steady line of men at the door. The letters were to wives,

107

girlfriends, and children. Some were short and matter-of-fact: "The weather was bad, but now it is better. I will see you in a few weeks." Others were full of longing and tenderness. Still others made her blush as she wrote.

She carefully addressed each one and put them into a pouch to be carried back. The men who could write brought their own letters.

Just as she finished, Daniel and Larson returned, carrying a heavy chest to Captain Nelson's quarters. Larson gave Hannah a look full of malice, but with the captain nearby he left quickly without speaking.

"I heard one of their crew say it was filled with Spanish doubloons," Daniel whispered as they returned to the main deck.

Hannah's eyes grew wide. A chest that size would hold a fortune. Daniel nodded, reading her thoughts. "I'm going to buy some land somewhere with my share. Have you given my idea any thought? We could be partners."

Ratso came up to them, saving Hannah from answering. "Mr. Gaines says we will drop the prisoners off on an island somewhere. Some of our crew will sail the *Lady Jane* back to Portsmouth. Her holds are full of sugar, coffee, spices, wool, and silk. The agent will sell it, and we will divide shares when we get back. The ship is a good one. Mr. Gaines says it can be refitted for our navy."

Captain Nelson picked ten men to sail the *Lady Jane* back to Portsmouth. "Mr. Gaines, you will be the acting captain. We will try to capture one more ship before we meet you at Portsmouth," he said.

Hannah was sorry to see Mr. Gaines leave the *Sea Hawk*. She knew that Captain Nelson had picked the most trustworthy and capable man to take the *Lady Jane* back to Portsmouth. Still, she wondered if the *Sea Hawk* would run as smoothly without him. Mr. Hailey, the second mate, was now the first mate. Hannah was not sure he could handle the crew, especially men like Larson. She had hoped Larson might be picked to help crew the *Lady Jane*; but, unfortunately, he was not. Neither was Daniel, Hannah was pleased to see.

Hannah wrote a quick note to Lottie and Madeline and tucked it into the pouch.

"Do you have a letter?" she asked Daniel.

Daniel's face darkened. "Sickness took my whole family. I am an orphan like yourself. Was a year ago when I was sixteen." He managed a smile. "That's why we should cast our lots together."

"Enough fun and games," Dobbs said from the hatch. "We've extra to feed tonight."

Hannah had forgotten all about her chores in the excitement. She hurried down to the galley after Dobbs.

She measured out the flour for the biscuits. "There are black specks in the flour," she said, peering closely. "Oh, it's weevils!" she cried when she saw them moving.

Dobbs shrugged. "Nothing we can do about that. They will die when they are cooked. It will just give the men some extra meat," he joked.

Hannah made up her mind not to eat another biscuit. She helped make a soup of dried peas and salt pork, and carried a pot of it and the biscuits to the prisoners.

The guards at the door kept their pistols ready. She looked curiously at the prisoners. In her mind, she had built the British to be monstrous killers. But these men did not look much different from their own crew. They seemed grateful for the good meal.

Hannah felt sympathy until she thought of the stories she'd heard about how the British imprisoned the American sailors on derelict ships until they died of starvation or disease.

By the time she had finished her chores, the *Lady Jane* had disappeared from view. Now that the excitement was over, Hannah felt disappointed. She knew the supplies would help the patriots, but capturing supplies from a merchant ship did not relieve the pain in her heart. She wanted to fight, not just be used as a tool to fool the enemy. But the thought of her "pretending" to be a girl almost made her smile. She sighed. Still deep in thought, she started across the deck, intending to go to her room. Suddenly, she felt something grab her ankle and looked down to see a rope wrapped around her foot. She took a hard fall, hitting the back of her head on the deck.

"You should watch where you are walking," Larson said mildly.

"You tripped me on purpose," Hannah sputtered with anger.

"Why, I did no such thing. I was just going to wind up this rope." He gave her a slow smile that dared her to prove otherwise.

Hannah looked around. Unlike Mr. Gaines, Mr. Hailey was nowhere in sight. Picking herself up with as much dignity as she could muster, she headed back to the galley. The sound of Larson's chuckling followed behind her all the way.

chapter eleven

Skulduggery

For a week, the *Sea Hawk* and its crew sailed in a calm and empty sea. The weather became increasingly warmer as they went farther south, and a gentle breeze sped them along. Hannah would have liked to sit on deck and enjoy the weather, but she never had time. From the moment she arose at daybreak until she fell exhausted into her hammock at night, she was busy.

The British prisoners added work for everyone. They were locked in the hold, and that required two sailors to stand guard. Hannah almost felt sorry for the prisoners. The hold was dark and smelly, and there were rats. Each day, the captain allowed the prisoners, two at a time, to walk about the deck for a short time. That required two more guards. Since the ship was already shorthanded, with ten of the crew sailing the *Lady Jane*, everyone had to do more than his share of work.

On every day except Sundays, if a sailor was found idle, some kind of work would be found, such as scraping the rails or repairing rope. Hannah looked forward to the short break at sunset. Daniel always sought out her company if he was free. Now that he knew she had lived on a farm, he was full of questions. He quizzed her about every aspect of farming. His eyes lit up when he talked about the farm he would one day own.

"What happened to your parents' farm?" he asked one night when they were talking.

Hannah was startled. "It's still there, I guess. The house and barn burned down."

"You should still own it," he said.

Hannah stared at him. Until that moment, it had never occurred to her. As her father's only heir, she probably could claim it. Then she shook her head. "I can't go back there. What if they came back?"

"The war won't last forever," Daniel said. "Is it good land?"

Hannah nodded. "My father said so."

"When it is over, we could go there. I could buy half and we could be partners. We could work hard and buy more land. Then when we both find wives, we could make a good life."

"Wives?" Hannah almost choked.

Daniel looked at her strangely. "Well, not right away. But someday."

She was not sure why the thought of Daniel with a wife made her feel so cross. "I'll think on it," she snapped.

A look of confusion and hurt passed over Daniel's face. Without another word, Hannah went back down to the galley.

Mr. Hailey did not keep the ship running as smoothly as Mr. Gaines had. Ropes were not always coiled away; decks were not as clean; even the rails needed to be scraped and painted. Several times, Captain Nelson spoke sharply to Mr. Hailey. Afterward, Mr. Hailey would curse and yell at some hapless sailor, but very little improved.

Because things on deck were so lax, Hannah was never sure if several incidents were caused by somebody's carelessness or were deliberate traps set by Larson. Ropes and equipment were left in her path. It happened often enough that she found herself looking nervously all around her every time she left the galley. After every mishap, she noticed that Larson was always nearby. That in itself was no proof, because usually he was exactly where he was supposed to be—on deck mending a sail, climbing the ropes, or carrying equipment. Sometimes he did not even seem to be watching her, although Hannah suspected he was. Other times he stared openly, chuckling softly. Hannah considered going to Mr. Hailey or even to

Captain Nelson, but she had no proof of her suspicions. For now, she remained silent, not confiding in Dobbs or even Daniel, who was becoming a good friend. Then, several days went by without an incident, and she began to breathe easier, thinking Larson had tired of his game.

The next day, some grease had been spilled on the steps going down to the hold. She nearly took a bad fall as she was carrying the midday meal for the prisoners. Surprisingly, Larson was nowhere in sight. Furious, she stormed back up to the deck. Larson was mending sails. He ignored her, seeming to be unaware of the angry looks she gave him. She went back to work, confused and angry. Was Larson doing these things?

She could not sleep that night. Troubled by her fear of Larson and a homesickness triggered by her talks with Daniel, she tossed and turned in her hammock. Sometime after midnight, she got up to visit the head. It was a quiet night. They were sailing through a light fog. Beyond the circle of pale light coming from the lantern at the wheel, the ship was dark. Hannah could hear the men on watch talking softly, but the fog made their shapes appear ghostly as they moved about the deck. Hannah was suddenly sure she was being watched, and she felt a chill of fear. She quickened her steps, trying to see her way in the fog. From somewhere close, she heard a stealthy noise that made her freeze. "Who's there?" she asked softly. Then something flew past her and landed with a twang in the wooded deck. She gasped in horror. It was a large knife. The handle still rocked back and forth, only inches in front of her. In fact, she realized with a growing panic, it was exactly where she would have been if the noise had not made her stop. She pulled the knife out of the wood, and holding it in front of her, hurried back down the hatch. She sat on her hammock, shaking, and listened for soft footsteps in the dark. It was almost daybreak before she at last fell asleep.

Dobbs examined the knife the next morning when Hannah told him what had been happening. "Why have you not mentioned this before," he asked with a concerned look.

Hannah shrugged. "I have no proof who it is."

"Someone should recognize this knife," he said thoughtfully. "Ask your friend Daniel. Or Ratso. They are in the crews' quarters where they might have seen it. "

"That's a good idea," Hannah said. She watched the men coming down to the crews' quarters for breakfast. Several men whom she did not know well passed, and then she saw Ratso. She motioned him aside and showed him the knife. "Do you know who that belongs to?" she asked.

Ratso nodded. "It belongs to that young fellow Daniel."

Hannah sucked in a breath. She felt like someone had hit her in the stomach.

"Are you sure?" she asked.

"Yes," Ratso said. "He showed it to me the first day when we were stowing our gear. Said his father gave it to him his last birthday. His father got sick and died right after that, so the knife is special to him. Want me to tell him you found it?"

Hannah shook her head. "Say nothing." At Ratso's puzzled expression, she added, "I want to surprise him."

"He won't hear it from me," Ratso said cheerfully.

Hannah set the tray for the captain. She was so distracted with her thoughts that she could hardly concentrate on what she was doing. How could it be Daniel? He was her friend. She had even been thinking of telling him she was really a girl. Why would he want to hurt her? A cold thought entered into her mind. He was so intent on getting a farm. Was he planning to kill her and somehow claim the farm for himself?

Dobbs put his hand on her arm. "I'm a pretty good judge of character. That boy is no killer."

Hannah jerked her arm away. "It was his knife," she said harshly. She picked up the captain's tray and headed up to deliver it.

"Things are not always what they seem," Dobbs called after her.

She did not answer. She was so lost in angry, confused thoughts that she did not even glance around for traps.

Right at that minute, she would have given almost anything to be back at the inn. There, she would have been safe with Madeline and Lottie, instead of on this ship with men who hated her for no good reason and others who pretended to be friends but were not.

The conversation between the captain and Mr. Hailey stopped suddenly when she entered the room. Both men stared at her as she laid out the captain's breakfast.

"Good morning, Jack," the captain said. He sounded less friendly than usual. "Are you not well this morning?"

"I'm fine, sir. I just did not sleep well last night." There was an awkward silence. For an instant, she considered telling them about the knife, but in the end, she remained silent.

She went to the captain's cabin to straighten it while he ate. She had just started to make his bed when the captain entered the room.

"Oh, I am sorry, sir. Do you want me to come back later?"

"No. Go ahead with your chores." He gave her a strange look.

"Is your breakfast not to your liking?" she asked.

"It's fine. Just do your work."

Hannah searched her mind for some reason for the captain's gruffness. Usually, he treated her kindly. An uncomfortable silence filled the room while she worked.

She was almost done when Captain Nelson said suddenly, "What kind of a man was your father?"

"A good man," Hannah stuttered, startled by the question. "A hard worker."

"Honest?"

"Yes, sir. Very," she answered.

"And did he pass these qualities on to you?"

"Yes, sir." Hannah remained puzzled. Did he have some special task for her? Something that would call for an especially honest person? She waited expectantly.

"If a person was overcome with temptation, what should he do about it?" Captain Nelson asked next.

"Do you mean like if someone stole something?" she asked. When Captain Nelson nodded, she said, "I imagine he should confess and try to make amends." She thought for a moment. "I would suppose that the sort of person who stole probably would not do that, though."

There was a sigh from the captain.

"Why are you talking this way, sir?" Hannah asked.

"You don't know?" He gave her a piercing stare.

Hannah shook her head, her stomach churning. He was not asking because he had a job for her; he thought that she was a thief. What could he possibly think she had taken? She looked about the room for something missing, and her gaze landed on the chest of doubloons.

The look was not lost on Captain Nelson. His eyes narrowed, and Hannah, suddenly sure what was missing, realized she had made herself look guilty.

Captain Nelson looked grave. "Go back to your chores. We will talk more of this later," he said, dismissing her.

"Sir, I—" Hannah began, but he turned his back on her until she left the room.

Hannah went about the rest of her chores in a daze. She gathered the dishes and washed them without a word. Although she had done nothing, just knowing the captain thought she was a thief made her feel guilty and worthless.

Daniel was swabbing the decks when she went to feed the animals. "Good morning," he said cheerfully. She did not answer, and after a minute, he turned away with a thinly veiled hurt look. Hannah looked after him. Wasn't she doing the same thing to Daniel as the captain had done to her? She hurried after him. "Daniel?"

He turned toward her, his expression cold. Hannah rushed in. "Do you have a knife?"

The joyful look on his face had to be genuine. "Did you find it? I lost it toward the beginning of our journey. Where did you find it?"

"Someone threw it at me," she said. "It just barely missed me."

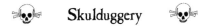

Emotions passed over Daniel's face—first dismay and concern, and then anger and disbelief. "And you thought it was me?"

"I didn't know what to think. Ratso said it was your knife," she said.

"So you thought I would throw knives at you?" Daniel asked again.

Hannah hung her head. "I'm sorry."

"I'm sorry, too," Daniel said. "I thought we were friends." He walked away without another word.

Hannah finished with the animals and went to her tiny room. She sat on her storage chest and put her head in her hands.

Dobbs stuck his head in the door. "Have you forgotten your duties?" He stopped. "Whatever is the trouble? Has someone tried to hurt you again?"

His kindness seemed to trigger the tears she had been barely managing to hold in. She sobbed, wiping angrily at her eyes, but unable to stop.

Dobbs knelt beside her. "A lad doesn't cry," he said gently. "But then you are not a lad, are you?"

chapter twelve

Thief

Hannah froze. What a terrible day it had been. The captain thought she was a thief; Daniel was angry with her; and now Dobbs had guessed her secret. She looked at Dobbs's gentle look of concern and sighed. "How long have you known?" she asked.

"I wasn't sure until this minute," Dobbs said. "I don't think anyone else suspects, though. You have done a good job of playing a boy."

"I tried to act like my brother, Jack."

Dobbs nodded. "Ah. So Jack is the real name of your brother, the one who died."

Hannah nodded. "You won't tell?"

Dobbs winked at her. "Tell what?"

Through the open hatch, they heard the call, "Land ho!"

Dobbs stood up and patted her head. "Dry your eyes. We'll talk later. The captain will pick a few men to go

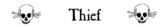

ashore and get fresh water. I'll wager you would like to step on land again."

"The captain won't pick me," Hannah said darkly. Nevertheless, she went up on deck. She was excited to see land again after all the weeks at sea.

"Looks like a good-sized island," Dobbs said, coming to the rail beside her. "There are some mountains," he said. "There's a good chance we can find fresh water. I would enjoy a cup of tea that wasn't slimy."

Hannah nodded in agreement. Stored in wooden barrels, the water on the ship had quickly grown stale and slimy, and it had a terrible odor. Tea and coffee did not disguise the foul taste.

They watched for a few more minutes, until Dobbs announced it was time to return to the galley and prepare lunch. "It will be a while before we anchor. Captain Nelson will want to get as close as he can, especially if we are going to be rowing heavy barrels of water. Mr. Hailey will have to take some soundings to see if the water is deep enough to go into that bay."

By the time the meals had been served and the galley cleaned, the island was plainly visible. Green trees, of a kind Hannah had never seen before, grew almost to the shore. The whole center of the island seemed to be mountains.

Hannah was just putting away the last pot when Mr. Hailey stormed into the galley with two other sailors. The officer's face was red with anger, and the men with him looked uncomfortable. Shoving Hannah aside, Mr. Hailey went to Hannah's small room. He glanced around quickly and then threw open the lid to Hannah's chest.

Hannah and Dobbs were so surprised that they stood speechless. At last, Dobbs found his voice. "What is the trouble, Mr. Hailey?"

"This is the trouble," Mr. Hailey shouted triumphantly, reaching in the chest and holding up a small bag. Hannah could hear the jingle of coins.

Hannah gasped in horror. "I don't know how those got there," she cried.

"By your thieving hand," Mr. Hailey said. "Captain Nelson will be glad to know I have solved the mystery," he added with satisfaction.

"How did you learn of this?" Dobbs asked.

"We suspected her all along, but I have found a witness who saw her sneaking out of the captain's quarters while he was inspecting the gun deck."

The two sailors, sympathetic a minute ago, roughly dragged Hannah up the stairs to the deck. Their faces were hard.

"Hold him there while I talk with the captain," Mr. Hailey ordered.

Hannah was the object of curious stares from her fellow crewmates as she stood there waiting. Her face burned with humiliation. Dobbs came up and stood nearby, as though to lend her his support.

Daniel came on deck and spoke quietly to Dobbs. After a short whispered conversation, Daniel nodded. Giving Hannah a quick smile, he went back down the hatch.

At last, Mr. Hailey emerged from the captain's quarters. Without a glance at Hannah, he went to the hatch and issued the call, "All hands on deck."

The men not already on deck poured out of the hatches. Ratso stood close, his wizened face frowning with concern. Larson was there, his face blank. His eyes met hers, and although he gave no sign, Hannah understood that he was the one who had put her in this position. Hannah searched the crowd of men. Where was Daniel? She did not see him. Then at last he emerged, giving Dobbs an almost imperceptible shake of his head.

Captain Nelson looked grim. "We are about to set anchor," he said, pacing the quarterdeck as he spoke. "I've touched on this island before. We can get fresh water and food. When we have taken our supplies, we will drop off the English. There is a village on the other side. Mostly descendants of the buccaneers who worked these waters a hundred years ago. It's a rough place, but they will eventually be rescued."

He paused in his speech and at last looked at Hannah. "We have another matter before us. The papers you signed when you came on board clearly stated the rules and the punishment for breaking them. Any bounty is to be divided among the crew in shares. If any man steals, he is robbing not only me but the whole crew. Unfortunately, this has happened. Our ship's boy, Jack, had access to the chest of Spanish doubloons. I suspected him, but Mr. Hailey has found proof. Jack, I sentence you to ten lashes, and you will be left on the island with the English."

The two men holding Hannah pulled her roughly to the rail and secured her hands tightly with rough rope. Glancing around her desperately, she saw that Daniel and Dobbs were not present. They had deserted her to a fate she had not earned. "Captain Nelson," she shrieked, "I did not do it! I swear to you!"

The captain had already turned to go back to his quarters, but he paused and turned toward her. "Then how do you account for the doubloons in your sea chest, Jack?"

"I can't," Hannah said miserably. "Someone put them there to make me look guilty. If I had taken them, would I be so foolish as to put them there? Especially after our talk this morning?"

Mr. Hailey was holding a whip, and he looked almost eager to dispense the punishment. Hannah knew she would

get no mercy from this man. "The punishment has been ordered," Mr. Hailey said.

Captain Nelson raised his hand to stop him. "Who on the ship would be such an enemy?"

"Mr. Larson," Dobbs's voice rang out from the hatchway. He held up a bag and shook it to show it was full of coins. "It was in the hold with the extra sails." Daniel stepped out from behind him and nodded.

"They are lying," Larson snarled. "They are both friends of the boy."

"I saw you coming out of Jack's room," Ratso suddenly spoke up. "Right when we first spotted the island."

Larson whirled and glared at the old man. "You couldn't have seen me. You were on deck with the others." There was a sudden silence. Larson, realizing what he had said, tried to cover. "We were all on deck."

One of the men holding Hannah spoke now. "No, I saw you go down the galley hatch. I wondered why at the time, because we were all so happy to see land again."

Another sailor spoke up. "I saw Larson going into the captain's cabin. I thought it was strange, because I knew the captain was not there."

Without waiting for the captain's orders, the men untied Hannah's arms and tied Larson in her place.

"I am sorry I doubted you, Jack," Captain Nelson said. "Mr. Larson, you will have the same punishment as Jack would have had for the theft. In addition, you will have five more lashes for your dealings with Jack."

Hannah's mouth was dry with relief and her legs shook so much she could hardly stand. She moved next to Dobbs and Daniel as Larson's shirt was removed. The whip cracked, and a red gash appeared on Larson's back.

"At least you have some revenge after all Larson did to you," Daniel said.

Larson stood, silent and defiant, as the whip landed again and again. Then his legs buckled and he screamed. Hannah turned away. "I have no stomach for it," she admitted.

Dobbs stayed on deck, but Daniel followed her down. "Thank you for helping me," Hannah said.

"I knew you were no thief," Daniel said. "Larson's bunk is right next to mine, so it would have been easy for him to take my knife. When Dobbs told me all the things Larson had been doing to you, I knew it had to be him. The coins weren't in his trunk, but then Dobbs thought about the sail room."

"I am sorry I doubted you," Hannah said. "I won't do that again." She paused. "I am going to trust you with a secret now."

Daniel looked at her curiously. "A secret?"

"I am a girl," she said simply.

chapter thirteen

The Island

Daniel's mouth dropped open. "Does anyone else know?" he asked, looking up toward the hatch where the last sounds of Larson's punishment could be heard.

Hannah nodded. "Dobbs guessed. You must not treat me any differently, or the others will know."

Daniel nodded quickly as Ratso came down the stairs. "You two better get up there. Captain's about to pick who goes on shore."

Captain Nelson named off ten men, including Daniel and Dobbs, to go ashore. Six men were to bring empty barrels and find fresh water. The other four were to cut firewood for the galley stove and look for fresh things to eat. Hannah was not named.

"Forgive me, sir," Dobbs said loudly. "Can I take Jack? He will be a big help to me finding food."

Captain Nelson nodded. The anchor was dropped, and the ship's two boats were readied. The water was clean, a beautiful shade of blue-green, and the breeze carried the scent of flowers. Although the men left behind were envious, none of them seemed to begrudge Hannah the chance to go ashore. They cuffed her and slapped her back. "That was a close call," one said. "Glad that scoundrel got showed up," said another.

Larson was gone, presumably locked up with the English sailors. Hannah looked at the island. She had wasted time feeling sorry for the prisoners. This was a paradise.

They rowed in two boats and beached them on a sandy shore. Hannah was one of the few who was not heavily armed. Seeing their pistols, muskets, and machetes, Hannah thought they looked like real pirates

Brown creatures jumped among the trees, making loud screeching noises. "What are those?" Hannah exclaimed in delight.

"Monkeys," Dobbs said, making a face. "Nasty things. They look cute, but they bite. If they are here, however, then so is fresh water. And food."

Mr. Hailey divided the men into two teams. "Don't use your weapons unless you absolutely must," he admonished. "No need to advertise that we are here." They left the barrels on the beach, and Mr. Hailey went with the men looking for water. Dobbs was left in charge of the wood and food.

"Let's tend to the firewood first," Dobbs said. He led his group, carrying axes, up a hill. It was rough going through the thick vines and vegetation, and they used machetes to clear a path.

"Look for logs that have already fallen," Dobbs instructed. "Green wood doesn't burn well." At last they found a huge tree, completely uprooted. Dobbs inspected it with a pleased look. "Must have come down in a storm." With two-man saws, they cut the tree into large pieces and rolled them down the path they had made. When they reached the beach, they split the large logs into small pieces that could be burned in the galley stove. Hannah's job was to stack them in one of the ship's boats. After several hours' work, Dobbs sent two men rowing the boat back to the ship. While they waited for the boat to return, Hannah and Daniel helped Dobbs catch several large turtles.

"The men will be happy with these," he declared. "Turtle meat is delicious."

Hannah felt sorry for the big lumbering creatures, but Daniel assured her Dobbs was right.

"You two take those buckets and pick some guavas," Dobbs ordered. He had pointed them out earlier. "They have a lot of seeds, but they're good. I'm going to look for some fresh greens."

Hannah was grateful for the time alone with Daniel. He had not said much since she had told him her secret.

They climbed a hill, using machetes to clear the way. After a few minutes, Daniel turned to her. "Is everything about you a lie then?"

"No, everything is true, except that it was my brother, Jack, who died."

"I'm glad you told me," Daniel said.

"You won't tell anyone?" Hannah asked.

Daniel shook his head. "I'll keep your secret. To tell the truth, I don't know how to act. I thought of you as a friend."

"We can still be friends," Hannah said. "Nothing has changed really."

Daniel laughed. "I think it has."

"I wanted revenge," Hannah said, "but I guess I wanted an adventure, too. I loved the farm, but sometimes I thought about my life. I would have married some neighbor boy and gone on doing the same things every day. I would have children and cook and clean and get old. I used to dream that I could do something exciting. Something I could think about while I was sewing and cooking. Do you understand?"

Daniel grinned at her. "So you decided to be a privateer and cook and clean instead."

Hannah laughed at herself. "Well, at least I have seen a little of the world. Like this island. It is beautiful here."

Daniel pointed to a knob of rock jutting out of the hill. "I'll bet if we could climb up there, we could see the other side of the island."

Hannah put down her bucket and laughed. "Race you," she said, already climbing and sending several monkeys leaping through the trees, screeching alarms.

They reached the rock at the same time. It was larger than they had thought and difficult to scale. Looking back, Hannah could see the beach far below, and off in the distance the *Sea Hawk* anchored in the turquoise waters. Hannah started to stand up, but Daniel suddenly pulled her down. "That's not fair," she protested. Then she saw the reason.

Daniel had been right. From their vantage point, they could see across the island. On the other side was a small town of maybe thirty houses. A narrow brown road wound around the end of the island to a wide bay. Silently, Daniel pointed to the harbor.

"It's the English ship that fired on us," Hannah gasped.

The ship lay at anchor. Its sails furled, the bare masts gleaming white in the bright sun. It was much larger than the *Sea Hawk* and painted blue, with a jaunty yellow stripe around it. Two of the ship's boats were pulled up on the sandy beach, near the road, but Hannah saw no sign of life.

"We have to warn Captain Nelson," Daniel said.

"I'll go," Hannah offered. "Someone should watch."

Daniel nodded. "Hurry!"

Going down the hill was nearly as hard as going up. The thick jungle vines seemed to have grown back, and Hannah was forced to cut her way free in several places, using her machete. She reached the beach just as Mr. Hailey arrived with his crew, rolling several barrels of fresh water.

While the men loaded the water in the boat, Hannah told him what they had seen. Dobbs came out of the jungle carrying a basket. He put it into the second boat and stopped to listen.

"Did you see any of the crew?" Mr. Hailey asked.

Hannah shook her head. "It's too far a distance to be sure. We might be able to see with the ship's glass."

Dobbs rowed with Mr. Hailey and Hannah in one of the small boats that was already filled with supplies. While the supplies were being unloaded, Hannah repeated her story to Captain Nelson.

"How close does the jungle come to the harbor?" he asked.

Hannah thought before she answered. "Nearly to the road. It's cleared some near the town."

"What do you think, Mr. Hailey?" Captain Nelson asked.

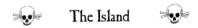

"Would be a prize for sure," the second mate answered. "But she is bound to have a larger crew. More than a hundred, likely."

"If they are all in town drinking, there may be only a few men on board," Captain Nelson said. "We need someone to take a closer look."

"I'll go, sir," Hannah answered. "I could take Daniel."

Captain Nelson looked at her thoughtfully.

"Gather the men on deck, Mr. Hailey," he said.

Most of the men were already on deck, enjoying a day of rest. When the last few joined them, Captain Nelson spoke. "The English ship is on the other side of the island," he said. "Common sense says that we slip away from here before she sees us. However, we have reason to believe that most of her crew might be away from the ship enjoying themselves in town. Jack and Daniel are going to see if we are right. The ship is a large frigate, twenty-four guns. Before we left port, General Washington was in dire need of gunpowder, and this ship is bound to have a good supply. As big as they are, I think they will not be expecting trouble. My plan is to wait until dark and sail as close as we can. We will take the longboats, row up to the ship, and sail her away. Of course, if we are discovered, or if there are more on board than we think, we could be in for a fight. So I put it to you. Shall we try to take her?"

A rousing cheer went up from the men. Captain Nelson turned to Hannah. "It is up to you. If the ship seems heavily manned, our plan will be too dangerous."

"We will find out," Hannah promised.

Dobbs came up from the galley with a small pouch. "There's food and water in there. Be careful, child," he said gruffly. "I've grown fond of you." He looked at her for a minute, then said loudly, "Captain!"

Captain Nelson looked up from giving instructions to Mr. Hailey.

"Jack here looks like a sailor. If he was wearing regular clothes, the English crew might think he was a town person, and the townspeople might think he was a passenger off the ship."

Captain Nelson nodded. "Good thinking, Dobbs. Have you any such clothes, Jack?"

Hannah shook her head, but Dobbs said, "He's not that much smaller than me. I've got some that will fit."

A few minutes later, Hannah, dressed in breeches, stockings, and a soft linen shirt, stepped into the boat. She carried the pouch of food and water and a change of clothing for Daniel.

"Now remember the story, lad," said Captain Nelson with a worried look.

"I'll remember, sir," Hannah said crisply. "You can depend on us. If the ship's crew sees us, we are the children of a cane plantation owner. If it is the townspeople, we are to pretend we came from the ship."

"You must be back before dark," Dobbs said. "You will never find your way through the jungle, and we dare not risk another day here."

Hannah nodded as she sat down in the small boat. As soon as they landed, she led Mr. Hailey up to the rock. Daniel was still watching, but he shook his head when they arrived. "It's just too far. I can't see anyone on board."

Mr. Hailey peered though the ship's glass. "Not even with this," he said in frustration. He lowered the glass and said, "Well, good luck, lads," and went back down the hill, occasionally hacking at the underbrush.

Hannah handed Daniel the clothes. Seeing his red face, she looked away and explained the plan while he changed.

"Let's be off then," Daniel said. Almost immediately, the jungle closed around them. The tall canopy of trees let only a small bit of light through to the ground. Because of the low light, few plants grew on the jungle floor, although it was difficult for Hannah and Daniel to pick their way over huge roots. Now and then, they had to use their machetes to clear the way. "It's so hot," Hannah groaned as they pushed their way up a steep hill. A large green lizard with bulging eyes scurried up a tree beside them. Hannah gasped in surprise.

"If it wasn't so miserably hot, it would be pretty here," Daniel said, pointing to some brightly colored birds.

"I have to stop for a minute," Hannah begged. Daniel nodded. Hannah tried not to think about snakes as they sat on a log from an old fallen tree and shared a drink from the canteen. "We have to keep going," Daniel said after a very short few minutes. "I don't think we are making very good time."

It was difficult to judge how far they had come or even if they were going in the right direction. After several hours, Hannah was drenched with sweat. Her arms ached from wielding the machete, and she itched from insect bites. Daniel looked every bit as miserable. Neither of them had the energy for conversation.

Then, thankfully, they seemed to be walking downhill. Daniel held out his arm so suddenly that Hannah stumbled into him. Just like that, the jungle had ended. Peering through the last few feet of vegetation, they could see the dusty road in front of them.

"The ship should be that way," Daniel said, pointing to his left. Keeping hidden, they skirted the edge of the jungle until they could clearly see the ship. Squatting down, hidden by some plants with large leaves, they observed the ship for several minutes. They could see the name on the side—the HMS *Majestic*.

"I can't tell anything," Daniel said in frustration. "I know there are men on board, but I can't tell how many."

"We need to go to that town," Hannah said. "At least close enough to see if a lot of the crew are there."

"You know we could be hanged as spies if we are caught," Daniel said quietly.

Hannah gulped, then nodded. In truth, she had not thought of that. Still, they had to get word back to the *Sea Hawk*.

"I've been thinking," Daniel said. "If we meet townspeople, we tell them we are from the English ship, and if the English sailors show up we say we are from the town. What if they are together? From what I saw, the town is so small they all know one another."

"Let's think of a better story," Hannah said as they walked, keeping under cover. "We could say we were captured by pirates, but when they found out we didn't have rich parents, they dumped us off on this island."

Daniel nodded. "What was the name of the pirate ship?"

Hannah grinned. "The *Sea Hawk*. It set sail yesterday."

"Let's hope we don't have to use any of those stories," Daniel said. The jungle was ending, and they could see fields of sugarcane. A sharp smell came from several buildings. "Rum," Daniel said, sniffing. "Let's hope they are selling a lot of it to the *Majestic*'s crew.

A new worry presented itself. The road suddenly veered away, obscured by the rum distillery. If they were going to continue into the town, they had no choice but to come out into the open.

Hannah and Daniel stood for a minute, and then each of them took a deep breath and stepped out of their leafy shelter. They walked past the cane fields to the road and followed it around the bend. Several black slaves looked up from their toil in the cane fields to stare at them curiously. Hannah and Daniel had to walk only a little farther before they could see the town, larger than they had thought. The first few houses seemed empty. An old dog snoozed on the saggy porch of one, and chickens pecked in the dusty yards. They could hear loud music now, and the sound of laughter. Suddenly a door opened, and a woman stepped out of one of the houses. She was dressed in a ragged but brightly colored dress and holding a large tankard. She stared at them and took a drink. "Harold," she called to someone inside, "We've got some visitors."

chapter fourteen

Pirate Adventures

Hannah froze, her heart pounding with fear. A man called out in a slurred voice from inside the house. "Who is it, then?"

The woman squinted at them, and Hannah realized that she was very drunk. The woman shrugged. "Just some boys."

"I don't care about boys," the man roared drunkenly. "Come pour me some more rum."

Daniel gave the woman a cheery wave. Guiding Hannah by the elbow, he pushed her up the street, away from the woman. Hannah sagged with relief. "I thought we were caught," she said.

"We still could be," Daniel said grimly. "I'd like to get a peek inside a few of those taverns and see if we can get a rough count of how many men are here."

They were in the main part of town, a cluster of faded whitewashed buildings that seemed to be mostly taverns. A church with a tall steeple looked out of place at the end of the street. They could see several ships, big enough to deliver rum to other islands, anchored in a small bay near the town. This part of the island had not been visible from their lookout, but now they could see several more prosperous-looking houses and plantations past the bay.

"Someone is having a good time," Daniel said quietly. From the taverns came the sound of music and loud voices.

A young man about Daniel's age, wearing a splendid blue uniform, sat on a bench outside one of the taverns.

Daniel approached him boldly. "Are you from that big ship?" he asked in a friendly voice.

The boy seemed glad for the company. He nodded. "The *Majestic*."

"We saw it. It looks like a fine ship," Daniel said pleasantly. "It sounds like half the crew is in there, though." He waved at one of the taverns.

The boy nodded. "More than half. We left only twenty men on board. I wish I were one of them."

"Why?" Hannah asked. "I would think you would be happy to spend a day on land."

The boy shrugged. "Not so lucky. My uncle is the captain. He's on the ship now, but at sunset he is coming ashore to have dinner at Mr. Henry's plantation." The boy paused and looked up at them. "Do you know him?"

Hannah shook her head. "We are just here visiting our uncle."

The boy nodded. "Mr. Henry is very rich. And," he added miserably, "he has four daughters. I have to go to dinner with them."

"That should be nice," Daniel offered.

"Nice!" the boy cried out. "I don't know what to say to girls. It also means that I have to stay neat and tidy until then, so I can't get drunk with the others."

"Then you will be saved a headache in the morning," Daniel offered.

"I have heard that girls like a fellow in uniform," Hannah told him. "Maybe they'll will be so thrilled with you that they will do all the talking."

The boy straightened his jacket, looking hopeful "Do you think so?"

"There cannot be many well-bred boys on the island," Hannah said. "The planter's daughters may all be competing for your attention. You might not have to say hardly a word."

The young midshipman looked pleased with this notion. "We have to go," Daniel said. "Our uncle is waiting for us. Will you be on the island long?"

"We set sail tomorrow," he answered.

"Too bad," Daniel said. "I would like to hear your story tomorrow."

Waving good-bye to the midshipman, Hannah and Daniel hurried through the town. In case the boy was watching, they headed toward the church and circled around to the cane fields and the jungle beyond. "We are great spies." Daniel grinned at her. He grabbed her hand and held it as they walked. Hannah was startled at first, but then she relaxed, enjoying the way Daniel's big hand felt so warm and safe covering her own.

"We have to hurry," he said as they plunged back into the steamy darkness of the jungle. "It is only about four hours until sunset. Captain Nelson will have to set sail around the island by dark. We will have to take the ship between dark and midnight."

A shiver of fear and excitement went down Hannah's back at the thought of taking the ship. Would she at last get a chance to fight the British? She thought about the earnest young midshipman. He had actually seemed quite nice. She was glad he would not be on the ship when they attacked.

The journey back was even worse, for now they were exhausted, and in the early evening, a sudden shower managed to get through the thick overhead canopy of leaves and drench them. It was nearly dark when they stumbled out of the jungle. Feeling enormously pleased with themselves, they rowed the small boat that had been left for them to the *Sea Hawk*.

"Captain Nelson is waiting for you," Mr. Hailey greeted them when they climbed on board. "He is in his quarters."

They found Captain Nelson pacing the floor. He looked pleased and relieved when he saw them. "Sit down, lads. Tell me what you found out," he said.

When they repeated the conversation with the midshipman, Captain Nelson beamed at them. "Well done!" he exclaimed. "I knew I could count on you. Now go and get yourselves something to eat and some well-deserved rest."

Dobbs was waiting in the galley with a bowl of turtle soup and a plate of greens and fruit. "This is delicious!" Hannah exclaimed.

"Don't get used to it," Dobbs said. "The fresh things won't last long."

Hannah and Daniel yawned at the same instant, making them laugh. "Get to your hammocks," Dobbs said.

"You will wake us when it is time to go?" Hannah asked.

"You have done your share for this prize," Dobbs said. "I doubt the captain will require you to be in the boarding party."

Daniel frowned. "I want to go."

"So do I," Hannah declared stoutly. She was not sure that was completely true. The thought of boarding the English ship and actually engaging in combat filled her with fear.

Dobbs sighed and shook his head. "I will wake you. But I have doubts that the captain will send you."

Hannah climbed in her hammock. It seemed that she had no more than closed her eyes when Dobbs shook her awake. Groggy with sleep, she swung out of the hammock.

"They just rowed the prisoners to shore," Dobbs said. "Larson, too. I doubt if he will get much acceptance from the English." He chuckled. "They were a pretty glum bunch when they left. I suspect their mood will be brighter tomorrow when they discover there is a town on the other side of the island."

It was fully dark. Hannah could see a pinprick of light from the beach where the released prisoners had managed to make a fire. She imagined them huddled around it, afraid and wondering how they would survive. In the morning, would they thank Captain Nelson for his kindness, or see that as a sign of weakness? She had not really thought about the new country they were making, but she suddenly felt proud to be an American.

Luck was with them. The clouds obscured the moon, and a light fog had risen. Captain Nelson spoke to the men. "From this point on we will maintain absolute silence and no light of any kind. Thanks to Jack and Daniel, we know there are about twenty men on board. We will put two boats over with about twenty-five men. With luck, we can take them by surprise."

Mr. Hailey started naming the men for the boarding party. "Sir, Jack and I want to go," Daniel spoke up.

"Jack is only a cabin boy," Mr. Hailey said.

"His parents were killed by the English, and he proved himself today," Daniel answered.

Mr. Hailey looked at the captain, who nodded. "I would not usually send one so young, but I need experienced men for the gun crews in case we have to fire."

Mr. Hailey opened a chest and passed out pistols, powder, and cutlasses. Hannah held her cutlass, surprised by its weight.

The winch was turned, pulling up the anchor. Mr. Hailey took his place along the rail with lead weights and rope to take soundings, because they would be sailing close to the shore.

Daniel patted her hand. "Are you afraid?" he asked.

Hannah's mouth was so dry she could scarcely speak. She nodded. Daniel smiled. "I am, too," he admitted in a whisper.

The fog was thick. It helped muffle the sounds—the creaking of the rigging, the soundings whispered by

Mr. Hailey, and the captain's commands to the man at the wheel.

Through the fog came a faint glow of light. They had reached the edge of the bay. Someone had hung two lanterns by the *Majestic*'s small boats, perhaps to light the way for the English captain when he returned. Hannah shivered. Would she have the courage to kill a man if it came to that?

The small boats were launched, and Hannah climbed down the ladder, awkwardly trying to balance the heavy cutlass. The rowers dipped their oars silently, paddling through the gloom. A faint glow from the ship's lanterns guided them, although when the fog lifted with a breeze, they were startled to see the ship suddenly looming over them.

Gasping, Hannah realized that they had nearly rowed right into the side of the ship. Quickly recovering, the rowers guided them around the ship to the stern. They would board near the captain's cabin. That area was forbidden to ordinary seamen, so they would have a better chance to board the ship without being discovered.

They had brought their own boarding ladders, but Mr. Hailey pointed without speaking. The boarding ladder was down, probably for the English captain's convenience, but it was like an invitation to them. Hannah tensed, waiting for the shout that meant somebody had discovered them, but still unseen they quietly climbed on board.

They were in a small hallway. The captain's quarters were on one side. Mr. Hailey drew his pistol and quietly entered. He returned a minute later. "Empty," he whispered. He divided them into groups to search the ship. "You two come with me," he whispered to Hannah and Daniel. "They are sure to have left a few officers on board. We will search all the officers' quarters."

The rest of the men slipped away in the fog. Drawing his pistol, Daniel opened the first door and crossed quickly to the bed. It was empty. The next room was also vacant. In spite of the chilly air, Hannah was sweating. From another part of the ship, she heard a quick shout and a bump. They reached for the third door when suddenly it opened, and a startled officer stepped out. "What is going on?" he demanded in a loud voice.

"We are taking your ship," Mr. Hailey said boldly. "Don't move, and we won't have to shoot you."

There was the smallest of sounds behind Mr. Hailey, and the English officer's eyes flickered to the dark hallway. Hannah turned in time to see a sword flash above Mr. Hailey's head. There was no time to think. Hannah swung her heavy cutlass up with all of her strength. There was a scream, and Hannah was suddenly splashed in blood. Their attacker clutched his arm, and Hannah realized she had completely severed his hand. It and the sword it had held fell on the floor, the fingers twitching uselessly. Filled with horror at what she had done, Hannah sagged weakly against the door.

The action had not completely stopped the downward motion of the man's sword. Mr. Hailey stumbled, grabbing at his shoulder trying to stanch the flow of blood. "He was going to cut my head off!" he exclaimed with a string of oaths. The first officer they had captured looked pale. Daniel kept his pistol pointed at him. "Get something to make a bandage," he ordered. He followed the officer into his room and watched as he pulled a soft cotton sheet from his bed. Using his knife, Daniel cut it into strips. Hannah helped Mr. Hailey pull off his shirt, wincing when she saw the wound. She made a pad to stop the flow of blood and wrapped the rest of the strip around tightly.

Daniel waved his pistol at the captured officer. "Help your friend," he said, handing him several more strips of cotton.

Leaving Daniel to guard the two officers for a moment, Hannah helped a pale and weak Mr. Hailey to the bed. When she returned, the British officer had applied a tourniquet to the wounded man's handless arm and the bleeding had slowed to a trickle. Hannah turned away. She was still in shock at what she had done.

Sounds of fighting were evident now, but already seamen from the *Sea Hawk* were climbing the rigging and making ready to sail.

Guarding their prisoners, they went out on the quarterdeck. Below them on the main deck, the remaining English crew were being gathered.

"What shall we do with them?" a voice asked.

"Throw them in the water. Let them swim to shore. It's not that far," Daniel suggested.

Several of the English sailors paled. Hannah thought of the man with no hand. "The wounded can't swim," she reminded him.

From far above came a cheerful melody. Whistling Sam, unfurling the topmost sail and forgetting the need for silence, was absentmindedly whistling. At that very instant, a shot rang out from behind one of the anchor winches. Whistling Sam jerked, his music silenced, and then fell like a stone to the deck. Another shot was fired, and a second seaman grabbed his arm but managed to hold on to the ropes.

Several men, Daniel among them, drew their pistols and ran to stop the British sailors. The officer they had captured made a move toward Hannah. She leveled her pistol at him. "Move again and you will be dead," she growled. There was a scuffle ending in a scream near the anchor. A second British sailor managed to shoot again before he was shot dead. The sailors from the *Sea Hawk* threw the two men's bodies into the sea.

Hannah looked at Whistling Sam, still lying where he had fallen. Only a minute before, he had been alive, whistling, pleased with the prize they had captured. Had the gunshot killed him instantly? Or had he known he was going to die as he was falling?

What did a man think about in those last few seconds of life? Hannah knew he had a wife and children. Had he thought of them? What had her parents and Jack thought in their last moments? Had her father regretted his stubbornness that had kept them from fleeing like everyone else? Had her mother regretted leaving Boston to make a home in the wilderness? And Jack? Had he mourned the life he would never have?

Life could end so quickly. Maybe instead of regrets, a person thought about the good things in life. Whistling Sam had been doing what he loved. Her mother and father had loved each other. Jack's life had been short, but she thought he had been happy. Maybe a person just had to live life the best he or she could every day.

Mr. Hailey crossed the deck and leaned weakly against the railing. His voice, however, was still strong. "Get those anchors up!" he shouted. With a worried look on his face, he strained to see the shore through the fog, which had returned. Hannah heard angry shouts and musket fire.

Through a break in the fog, she could see men running for the boats beached on the shore.

Then from the *Sea Hawk* came a deafening roar. The men on the shore retreated as a cannonball streaked over their heads and crashed onto the road.

The *Majestic* began to glide away, and the men let out a rousing cheer. Hannah looked at Daniel and saw him cheering with the others. He looked up and smiled.

"What's going to happen to us?" one of the English sailors asked.

The officer with them shook his head. "We can't look for mercy from a band of pirates," he said.

Mr. Hailey overheard him. "From a band of pirates, no. But from American privateers, yes. The *Sea Hawk's* boats are tied to the stern. Captain Nelson gave orders to release you without harm. Take your men and row to shore," he told the *Majestic's* officer.

The officer looked as if he could not believe what he had heard. "You are not keeping us prisoners?"

"We have no time for that," Mr. Hailey said, standing proudly in spite of his wound. "We have a war to win and a country to build. Give us some time, and we will be the greatest nation on earth."

The English officer shook his head. "I doubt it," he said.

"I believe it," Daniel said from beside Hannah.

"I do, too," Hannah said.

"Jack," said Mr. Hailey. "We are going to need a cook. Can you handle that, do you think?"

"Yes, sir," Hannah answered briskly. She started down to inspect the galley. Then she stopped and motioned to Daniel to come over to her. She whispered to him so Mr. Hailey and the rest of the crew could not hear. "No matter how many British I wound or kill, my family is not coming back. I think that when we get back to Portsmouth, I will see if Lottie and Madeline will let me come back to the inn."

Daniel's face fell. "I thought we might . . . " He stopped whispering, looking embarrassed.

"You didn't let me finish." Hannah smiled. "When the war is over, maybe we could go back to my farm."

"We would have to get married," Daniel said, making his whisper even more inaudible. "You being a girl and all."

Hannah laughed. "Maybe someday. But as Mr. Hailey said, first we have a war to win and a country to build."

the end

The Real History Behind the Story

Almost as soon as men sailed the sea in ships, there were pirates. Julius Caesar is reported to have been kidnapped and ransomed as a young man. Most people, however, consider the sixteenth and seventeenth centuries—the age of men such as Blackbeard, Captain Kidd, and Calico Jack—to be the golden age of piracy.

Slow-moving Spanish galleons, heavily laden with treasure, made easy targets for pirates based in the Caribbean. Governments offered pardons and sent ships to stop them; but for nearly two centuries, pirates plundered merchant ships in the Caribbean and along the Atlantic Coast of America.

Pirate ships were run like a democracy. The crew voted on a captain (and could vote him off). Articles—listing the ship's rules, division of the spoils, and even payment for wounds in battle—were drawn up and signed by all of the crew. One rule that all ships had was no women. In fact, a man sneaking a woman on board could be put to death. Women were considered bad luck on ships, and since most pirates were young (in their twenties), women on board could cause jealousy and friction.

Seamen needed to be good climbers so that they could lash and unfurl sails.

Anne Bonny (left) dressed in men's clothes to escape her husband and begin a life of piracy. Mary Read (bottom), also disguised as a man, later joined her on the ship.

For this reason, there were few women pirates. Two notable exceptions were Anne Bonny and Mary Read. Both women had worn men's clothing for much of their lives. Both sailed with Calico Jack. When they were captured, the women put up a ferocious fight, while the men were drunk below. Calico Jack was hanged, but the judge spared the two women, each was expecting a child. Mary Read died in prison either before her baby was born or during childbirth, but Anne Bonny's fate is unknown.

Unlike real pirates, privateers were licensed to prey on another country's ships. With a letter of marque, they would not be hanged when captured, but treated as prisoners of war. Often this was an even worse fate. The British held their prisoners on derelict ships, where most prisoners died from starvation, cold, and disease.

The American colonies used privateers in their fight for independence. The new government had few ships in the newly formed navy and was desperate for gunpowder and other supplies. Merchant ships like the *Sea Hawk* were outfitted to become privateer ships. They carried much larger crews than ordinary merchant ships. Privateers often captured ships by trickery and intimidation. Although Americans had prison ships, the soldiers and sailors were kinder to their prisoners, often letting them go with a promise not to fight against them again.

There is some evidence that women did sail on some of these ships. John Paul Jones, mentioned in Hannah's story, is reported to have had a black woman cook. Names of women appear in ship logs suddenly, as though they had just been discovered. In fact, several women sailed in disguise on British ships long enough to draw a pension.

Joseph Brant, who spares Hannah's life in the cave, was a real person. His Iroquois name was Thayendanega, and he was highly educated and a convert to Christianity. (Many colonists called American Indians "savages" because they were not Christian.) Brant made several trips to England seeking compensation for the Iroquois' service to the British.

Ships at sea were often caught in storms. The crewmen of such a ship would have to risk their lives on deck to make sure the vessel did not sink.

In Boston, Hannah meets Paul Revere. The real Paul Revere fought in the French and Indian War, then came home to run the family silver shop. He was married twice and had eight children by each wife. Paul Revere became famous when Henry Wadsworth Longfellow wrote his poem "The Midnight Ride of Paul Revere" about Revere's journey to warn colonists that the British were coming. However, what most people do not know is that three men made that ride, each from a different direction, to make sure the message was delivered. Paul Revere was briefly arrested, but he was set free.

The Portsmouth Flying Stagecoach was also real. It was one of the first regular stagecoach lines in the country. It was started by an innkeeper named John Stavers and his brother, Bartholomew, who was the first driver. Bartholomew was loyal to England. He returned to England, leaving his wife and unborn son. John came under suspicion and was briefly held prisoner, but signed an oath of loyalty.

In Portsmouth, Hannah meets John Paul Jones. He was indeed a notorious ladies' man but also a fierce fighter. His ship, the *Ranger*, was actually built for another captain. The builder did not like John

Paul Jones, and they argued about how to outfit the ship. Jones sailed across the Atlantic, and burned and sank ships along the coast of Ireland. Later, on another ship, the *Bonhomme Richard*, Jones spoke his famous words, "I have not yet begun to fight," when asked to surrender. He, other members of the Continental Navy, and—of course—the brave American privateers helped in the effort to defeat the British.

John Paul Jones is known as the Father of the American Navy.

Further Reading

If you would like to read more about pirates and privateers, here are some interesting books.

Fiction

Gilkerson, William. *Pirate's* Passage. Boston: Trumpeter, 2006.

Lee, Tanith. *Piratica: Being a Daring Tale of a Singular Girl's Adventure Upon the High Seas*. New York: Dutton Children's Books, 2004.

Meyer, L.A. *Under the Jolly Roger: Being an Account of the Further Nautical Adventures of Jacky Faber*. Orlando, Fla.: Harcourt, 2005.

Rees, Celia. *Pirates! The True Remarkable Adventures of Minerva Sharpe and Nancy Kington, Female Pirates*. New York: Bloomsbury, 2003.

Strickland, Brad, and Thomas E. Fuller. *The Guns of Tortuga*. New York: Aladdin Paperbacks, 2003.

Nonfiction

Cooper, Michael L. *Hero of the High Seas: John Paul Jones and the American Revolution*. Washington, D.C.: National Geographic, 2006.

Matthews, John. *Pirates*. New York: Atheneum, 2006.

Platt, Richard. *Pirate*. New York: DK Publishing, 2004.

Sharp, Anne. W. *Daring Pirate Women*. Minneapolis: Lerner Publications Company, 2002.

Internet Addresses

About.com: Female Pirates

<http://womenshistory.about.com/od/femalepirates/Female_
   Pirates.htm>

**Maritime Service Veterans: Privateers and Mariners in the
   Revolutionary War**

<http://www.usmm.org/revolution.html>

Privateers in the American Revolution

<http://www.nps.gov/revwar/about_the_revolution/privateers.
   html>